About the author

Sue Brady was born in the mid-1950s. She spent her childhood and teenage years in Cambridgeshire, before moving to Norfolk when she married. She lives thirty miles from Norwich with her husband, two children and three grandchildren. This is her debut novel.

PRECIOUS GEMS

Sue Brady

PRECIOUS GEMS

Vanguard Press

A CIP catalogue record for this title is
available from the British Library.

ISBN 9781784656485

*Vanguard Press is an imprint of
Pegasus Elliot MacKenzie Publishers Ltd.*
www.pegasuspublishers.com

First Published in 2020

**Vanguard Press
Sheraton House Castle Park
Cambridge England**
Printed & Bound in Great Britain

Dedication

For Mum and Dad who would be proud
'I went for it!'

Acknowledgements

Thank you to everyone who has taken this fantastic journey with me, all the staff at Pegasus for their unwavering support and my family and friends for their patience and endless cups of tea!

Chapter 1
November 1945

"Come on, Pearl, are you ready?" Ruby Williams stood shivering on the Millers' doorstep as the drizzly November weather was closing in. "Don't forget the tickets!" she called out as she hugged herself in her good navy wool coat. She checked her stocking lines were straight and hoped Pearl wouldn't take long otherwise her mum, Gwen, would invite her in and, as much as she loved Pearl's parents, they would never get away and she was eager to get dancing.

"Yes, I'm coming, hang on while I find my scarf. My hair will just go flat unless I cover it until we get there. The tickets are in my bag," replied Pearl, hurriedly putting her coat on and tying her silk scarf around her blonde curls, checking her bag to make sure she had the tickets at the same time. She shouted goodbye and closed the door of the semi-detached house she shared with her parents. A muffled 'Have fun and behave' came back from her dad, John.

They were off to the dance at the town hall in Norwich; there was a band playing tonight and they were looking forward to a night out.

"We're meeting up with Sandra and Margaret later," Ruby said. "They said they would be a bit late as Sandra had to run a couple of errands for her mum, so I said we would meet them there."

They had been friends since Ruby's parents had moved to Norwich nine years earlier; Ruby had been seated next to Pearl on the first day of term in tutor class as the teacher had said two precious gems should be together!

They had looked at each other shyly and then Ruby grinned at Pearl and said hello and that was it, they instantly hit it off, they went to the refectory for lunch together where they chatted and found out about each other. Pearl was a shy nine-year-old and Ruby a livelier eight-year-old. They discovered they only lived two streets away from each other, not too far from the beautiful cathedral. They were both only children and spent all their time after school with each other from that day on. They did their homework together and woe betide anyone who tried to bully Pearl; Ruby was her fiercest ally. They remained firm friends even when they left school, Pearl taking a secretarial job in an insurance office and Ruby with a similar role in the local solicitors' office. Working the same hours meant they were able to meet up for lunch and a gossip most days.

"Is Margaret still seeing Percy?" asked Pearl as they made their way into the High Street, their teeth chattering as the cold started to set in and their heels clicking on the wet pavement.

"I don't know," Ruby said, "The last I heard she was getting a bit fed up with his drinking, always out with the lads and no time for her."

The war was finally over, and everyone was trying to adjust and gain some level of normality back in their lives; people were partying and enjoying themselves to get rid of the horrors they had been through. Nearly every family they knew had lost a loved one or been touched by the war in some way.

"Well, Percy hasn't got over losing two of his older brothers right at the end of the war and his mother is completely heartbroken, so I suppose it's his way of dealing with everything," Pearl said.

"Yes, you're right," said Ruby. "But I'm not sure Margaret sees it like that, she wants to know if his intentions are honourable and she's hoping they will get engaged soon. She's always been a bit selfish, but this time I think she's right and he can't keep messing her about. She's been writing to that soldier she signed up as pen pal for, what was his name? I can't for the life of me think of it."

"Hmm, Godfrey? Gordon? No, Geoffrey! That's it!" Pearl said. "Do you think she'll meet up with him when he gets back then? That will ruffle Percy's feathers!"

"Ah! Yes, Geoffrey! Well, he's not stationed around here but I heard they are putting on special trains for people to get home etc. so I think they will find a way if it's meant to be. If Percy doesn't sort himself out, she'll be off, you mark my words!" said Ruby emphatically,

"Right, here we are. Anyway, don't mention anything to either of them or I'll be the one in trouble," Ruby giggled as they drew nearer.

There was a queue to get in and Pearl fumbled around in her bag for their tickets as they waited in line. "Is my lipstick all right?" she asked, pouting at Ruby in the lamplight, her blue eyes looking navy in the light.

"Yes, it looks lovely – as always. Quick, take off that scarf, we're moving," Ruby said as they shuffled up the line. Pearl whipped off the scarf and shoved it in her coat pocket, shook out her blonde curls and prayed they would last the night. Her mum had put them in rollers the night before for her and it was torture trying to sleep with the pins digging in her scalp every time she turned over. Still, it was worth the end result; she loved the feel as they bounced about her shoulders.

Ruby had long lustrous brunette hair which never seemed to need any work on it. It always looked healthy and had a natural curl to it, and with her warm chocolate eyes she was looking beautiful tonight. Pearl sighed inwardly with envy but satisfied herself with the thought that her bust was bigger than Ruby's, so the lads wouldn't just be looking at her hair! She adjusted the sweetheart neckline of her new red dress under her coat to make sure as they reached the front of the queue.

Pearl was eighteen and Ruby had just turned seventeen. Technically they weren't really allowed in as the legal age for drinking was twenty-one, but they looked older than their years with their sophisticated hair and make-up. The man on the door glanced at them and recognised Pearl, he knew her dad, "Hello, love," he said, "Say hello to your dad for me." He winked at the girls and tore their tickets in half and gave them the numbered stubs back. "Keep that for your coats," he said, "There's a raffle tonight so when you hand in your coats, you'll be given a raffle ticket – don't lose it, first prize is a bottle of whisky!"

He wasn't really that bothered about checking to see if the young ones were old enough to get in, he knew well enough they needed some fun back in their lives and the barmen would keep an eye on the drinking so there wouldn't be any trouble inside.

"Phew! That was close." Ruby and Pearl giggled together as they made their way to the coat station. "I thought he was going to bar us when he realised he knew my dad," Pearl said with relief they had made it in.

The band hadn't started yet, but as they were setting up a record player was playing some music to listen to. The bar was getting busy and everyone was standing around chatting, tapping their feet to the music and having a look to see who was coming in next through the doorway.

After the band had played the first couple of songs, the girls were getting a drink and chatting to Sandra and Margaret who had just arrived. "Don't look now but that group of lads is watching us," said Ruby, and immediately all the girls' eyes swivelled about. "I said don't look!" she admonished. "I like the look of that one," she giggled and smiled flirtatiously at one of the boys. Even though Ruby was a year younger than Pearl she was much more daring and confident, especially when it came to be chatting to the boys and she was soon dancing and flirting with Johnny, the boy she had liked for some time.

Pearl stood and watched her. Ruby's green shimmery dress swirled around her shapely figure as she moved to the music. Enviously, Pearl stood and tapped her feet on the edge of the dance floor and hoped she didn't look too much like a wallflower.

Sandra and Margaret stood with her for a while and then Margaret spotted Percy arriving; they made their way over to him and his friends. Pearl was going to join them but decided instead to wait for Ruby when the music had stopped.

Edward Turner was twenty years old and had returned home from the war relatively unscathed, but some of the memories would remain with him forever he was sure. He was with a gang of lads who stood around the edge of the dance floor near the bar looking at all the girls in their best frocks.

He wasn't the tallest in the group, but he was broad shouldered and, with his black hair slicked back, he had a look of Tyrone Power, the American movie star, about him – or so he had been told. He had noticed Pearl earlier as she had stood with her friends and now, after

16

a couple of beers, he saw her on her own and he found the courage to approach her. Edward came over and shyly asked Pearl if he could buy her a drink. She looked him up and down and took pity on him as he seemed so nervous and said she would love a gin and tonic.

"Righto, I'll be as quick as I can," he said with a big grin on his face, his walk to the bar had a slight swagger as he was rapidly gaining confidence. He introduced himself as he handed Pearl her drink, "I'm Edward, Edward Turner," he said, then rushed on, "I wasn't sure if you wanted ice, so I asked them to just put one cube in, I hope that's all right?" The nerves were back as he faced her.

"I'm Pearl Miller," she said smiling at him, "It's perfect, thank you." Pearl sipped her drink casting shy glances at Edward; after a couple more drinks she and Edward took to the dance floor as the band played a Glenn Miller song, *A String of Pearls*, which Edward said would be 'their song' from now on. Pearl was glowing with delight, deciding she really liked this boy, he was so attentive and seemed to like her too! They danced together for the rest of the evening, oblivious to anyone else.

Over the following weeks Pearl and Edward had several dates and soon became a couple. Ruby was delighted her friend had met someone and teased Pearl endlessly about when they were getting engaged. Pearl and Edward had been inseparable since that first date and it came as no surprise to everyone that they were engaged by Easter the following year, with Edward producing a beautiful sapphire ring after nervously asking her dad for her hand in marriage. Her parents were delighted as they liked Edward very much. They happily gave their blessing and held a small party to celebrate.

Ruby was so excited for them and constantly made Pearl promise she would be the chief bridesmaid for their wedding which was to take place the following year.

"I have to be the chief bridesmaid!" said Ruby pouting at Pearl, "Friends to the end – don't forget!" It was something they had said all through their schooldays and Ruby still said it now.

When they married a year later on a beautiful July day, Ruby was indeed the bridesmaid. Pearl looked lovely in the dress her mum and aunts had made from the parachute silk one of her uncles had managed to get hold of and Ruby looked adorable in a lovely peach dress.

They were all so happy and had their whole lives to look forward to.

Chapter 2
May 2018

"Pearl? Pearl! Wake up, dear!" She could hear someone calling her and a gentle rocking on her shoulder. "Pearl?" Pearl's eyes snapped open and she looked about her confusedly. "You must have nodded off then for a minute," said Jill, the auxiliary care worker at Willow Lodge Retirement home, plumping up the cushion at Pearl's back and readjusting her glasses.

"Ooh, no, I only just shut my eyes for a second," said Pearl indignantly as she slowly came back from the snooze. Her face was lined and wrinkled; her skin all crêpey and papery now; her blues eyes were faded but still retained the sparkle she had from her younger days. "Are they here yet? Do I look all right? Is my lipstick smudged?" She patted her soft wavy hair, styled by Sheila, the local hairdresser who normally came in once a week, but had made a special visit for Pearl the day before.

Pearl had moved into Willow Lodge ten years ago and she was happy and contented there. She had lived alone for eight years after Edward's death in 2000 and, when her children had gently suggested she would be more comfortable and have some company in a retirement home, she had eventually agreed. It was a hard wrench to leave her home, but it was getting harder to manage the house by herself now she was getting on and she knew now she had made the right decision.

Willow Lodge had fifteen rooms with ten solely for long-term residents and the other five were used for short-term recuperation, with patients coming in to recover from operations or respite care. Occasionally family members had stayed in one of the short-term rooms when a resident was ill or getting close to the end of their life.

"No, not yet, they should be here in about ten minutes, so don't worry, I just thought you might like to freshen up first." She handed Pearl a wet wipe for her face and hands and Pearl got out her handbag mirror to check everything was fine; she re-applied her lipstick and was finally ready. Pearl had worn the same shade of lipstick since she was old enough (and allowed to) wear it – Elizabeth Arden Victory Red – she loved it.

Pearl adjusted her pastel lemon scarf with tiny bluebirds on it around her neck and smoothed the front of her blue dress. Jill smiled fondly at the ninety-year-old. "You look beautiful, Pearl, and your lipstick is perfect. Are you looking forward to seeing everyone?"

"Hmm, stuff and nonsense if you ask me!" said Pearl, putting her lipstick back in its little holder and into her handbag, "Who cares if it's my ninetieth birthday? I've had so many now I can't be bothered to keep blowing out all the blasted candles – I'm sure I'm going to lose my teeth one day!"

"Ha, ha," said Jill, her pretty cornflower blue eyes twinkling at Pearl. "You know you enjoy these get togethers really and I'm sure everyone will love to see you blow your candles out. You never know, if you're really lucky you might have a bit of a dance when the music gets going. It will be fun and do you good."

Pearl looked at the young woman in front of her and sighed. "Yes, I do really. You are right and sorry if I'm a bit grumpy, dear, I just feel so old!"

The truth was that Pearl had been spending more and more time thinking about her Edward. He'd passed away eighteen years ago, and she missed him more now than ever. She was looking forward to being with him again when the time came, and it was increasingly becoming more difficult not to want that time to hurry up.

She seemed to spend more time reminiscing about their life together and remembering the good times they had. It was easier to remember things that had happened forty or fifty years ago than it was to remember what she had for lunch the day before!

The sound of cars on the gravel outside the home brought Pearl back from her reverie. The front door opened, and a cacophony of chatter and laughter filled the hallway before they all spilled into the lounge where Pearl was waiting; "Hello, Mum," said her daughter Susie fondly as she rushed over to kiss her cheek.

"Happy Birthday! How are you?" At sixty-eight Susie was still a striking woman with blonde hair and blue eyes and a slim figure. As usual she was immaculately dressed, wearing a fitted cream top and tan trousers with soft tan loafers on her feet. Everyone said she looked exactly like Pearl when she was younger, which Susie took as a huge compliment.

"I'm fine thank you, darling, it's lovely to see you," replied Pearl, holding onto her daughter for a hug. Susie's husband Dan gave his mother-in-law a warm embrace and cast about looking for somewhere to sit.

"Mum, Hi, Happy Birthday!" said Pete, her son and older than Susie by four minutes. Having twins was a blessing and a nightmare at the same time, but now they were older they seemed to be closer than ever and Pearl was happy to see them together.

"Hello, darling," said Pearl, gazing at her son with his faded blond hair showing greyer (Susie paid a fortune at the hairdressers for her lustrous shade!) and the same baby blue eyes as Susie.

They had both been dark haired when they were born and Pearl had thought they would take after Edward, but their hair gradually lightened to blonde as they grew up.

Pete was wearing his signature outfit of loose-fitting chinos and a polo top. Since retiring three years ago, he had decided he wasn't going to wear a suit ever again if he could help it!

Pearl looked around and saw her grandchildren waiting with arms loaded up with presents and flowers.

Susie's eldest daughter Caroline came over to hug her grandmother and deposited a large bouquet in her arms. "Lovely to see you, Grandma, you look beautiful. That scarf Milly got you is perfect with that dress!" Caroline took after her father and was taller than Susie, but at forty-seven she had the same elegance as her mother.

Caroline and Tim had two children; Milly and Simon. Milly was pregnant with her second baby and was currently negotiating her way through the room in a long floaty maxi dress holding hands with little Harry who, at two-years-old, was a cheeky, chubby bundle of fun. "Great-Grandma, you look amazing!" said Milly, gratefully plopping down in the comfy chair next to Pearl.

"Hello, sweetheart, how are you? When are you due?" Pearl asked, keeping one eye on Harry as he started fiddling with her bracelet dangling from her arm.

"Six more weeks yet," said Milly, trying to get comfortable. "I'm on maternity leave now so I'm resting a bit more, unless this little hooligan plays me up!" She squeezed Harry and he collapsed into fits of laughter. "Sorry Scott couldn't make it, but he sends his love and we'll pop down again once the baby arrives."

"Ah, that will be lovely, darling, I'll look forward to it and I know Betty in the room next to me has been knitting away ferociously so I'm sure there will be several little matinee jackets and whatnot to come," said Pearl. "She's so sorry to have missed you, but her family have taken her out for the day. She said to pass on her best wishes, and she hopes you like the things she's made."

"Oh, that's so kind of her." Milly was touched by her thoughtfulness. "Please tell her I said thank you and when this baby arrives – if it ever does – she can be one of the first to have a cuddle, after you of course, Great-Grandma!"

Simon, at twenty-two, was younger than Milly by two years. He was single at the moment, having broken up with Bryony a couple of months ago. He was enjoying his freedom and in no particular hurry to find anyone else. Tall and slim, he strode over to kiss Pearl. "Hi, Gran, you look beautiful as always! he said.

"Oh, darling, thank you, apart from all the grey and the wrinkles you mean?" said Pearl, laughing fondly at her great-grandson.

"What grey? Surely your hair is all natural?" He winked at Pearl as her hand flew up to pat her dyed blonde hair. It was very subtle; nothing too brash, she knew she should probably just let it go completely grey or it might even be pure white by now, but she hung on to that last little bit of vanity – well, that and her beloved lipstick!

Susie's second daughter Fleur came over next and bent down to hug Pearl; "Ooh, Grandma, I love that perfume, what is it?" she said as she sniffed Pearl's wrist.

"Hmm, I can't remember the name of it now – Josh's Emma brought it for me yesterday. Your mum might know though," Pearl said, fondly. Fleur was a lively forty-three although she looked and acted a lot younger – she often teased her sister that having no children had kept her so young looking!

She and her husband Nick had recently returned from living in New York where Nick's job had been based. They were now back living in the UK and had bought a lovely house in Swaffham.

"You must tell me all about your new house, dear," Pearl said. "Are you all settled in now?"

"There's still a fair bit to do, decorating and so on, but we are getting there, I'll show you some photos later, mmm… I really like that smell. I'll give Emma a call tomorrow, when they are home from the wedding and ask her what it is, I love it!" Fleur said, breathing in the scent again.

Josh at thirty-nine was Susie's youngest. He and his wife Emma were going to a wedding today and as he was best man and their teenage daughter Shannon was a bridesmaid, they couldn't fit in Pearl's party as well, so they had come down to see Pearl the day before and had a little celebration with her.

"You can check in my room if you like, darling, it's on the dressing table," Pearl said to Fleur fondly. "I'm sure Jill won't mind if you just pop in and out."

"Hee, hee. Okay, it's the one on the right isn't it?" giggled Fleur. "Shan't be a mo. – keep your eye out, Grandma!" She raced off in the direction of Pearl's room and was back in a flash.

"No one saw me!" she said, returning breathlessly. "It's called 'Spring Blossom'."

"Ah, that's it!" said Pearl, "I couldn't remember!"

"I had a quick squirt! Here, sniff my wrist, does it smell the same on me?" asked Fleur, thrusting her arm under Pearl's nose.

"Lovely." said Pearl, "I'm sure Emma would get you some or let you know where she bought it. It is lovely, it's not too overpowering and it doesn't smell like cat's wee!"

Fleur started laughing, "Ha, ha. Yes, I know exactly what you mean, Grandma, some of them smell like that on me too!"

"Is anyone else coming or is this everybody?" Pearl asked, looking around and pleased everybody had made the effort to come and see her. "I think Michelle and Jill have organised some drinks – oh, hello, Ted, come on in and meet everyone."

Ted, one of the residents, had come in and brought Hilda and Arthur with him. They were all long-term residents of Willow Lodge and good friends with Pearl.

"Well, bugger me, you've a lot of family here, Pearl," Ted announced happily, helping himself to a drink from the tray near the door. "Yes, definitely a good bunch!" he said appreciatively.

"I think we are all here now," said Susie, glancing surreptitiously over at Caroline and Dan. They took the hint and rushed off to make sure Jill and the team had organised the candles on the cake.

Michelle, one of the carers, came over to Pearl and discreetly took the flowers. I'll just pop these in some water for you, Pearl," she said.

"Oh, yes, thank you, dear." Pearl gave her the flowers and was rubbing at a tiny damp patch the flowers had left on her dress.

The lights dimmed and Pearl looked round expectantly.

"HAPPY BIRTHDAY TO YOU, HAPPY BIRTHDAY TO YOU," they all sang as Jill came through carrying the beautifully iced cake Susie had brought. The candles burned brightly in the dimmed room with a large nine and zero in the middle.

Pearl was just about to blow them out to a chorus of "MAKE A WISH, GRANDMA" from the younger ones, when she peered ahead of her and had to look again. She stood frozen, as there in the gloom, slowly making her way into the room with two sticks and a helper was Ruby!!

Everyone started to clap as the two old friends embraced one another for the first time in at least eight years.

"I didn't think I was going to see you again," Ruby said, crying softly as she stood with Pearl's arms around her.

"Oh, you silly thing, of course we'd see each other again. I have missed you though, it's been too long," chided Pearl, her eyes glistening with tears.

"I've bought you a little something," said Ruby, handing over a small package. Her chestnut eyes were shining too.

"Ah, you didn't need to buy me anything, Ruby, but thank you, dear." She carefully tore off the paper and inside was a small box with a pair of pearl earrings inside. "Oh, Ruby! They are lovely, they will go perfectly with my necklace. I'll ask Jill to help me put them in later, thank you so much." The two friends embraced again warmly.

"Right," said Pete eagerly. "Come on, Mum, blow out these bloody candles before the place catches fire and let's get this party going!" Everyone cheered and clapped as Pearl managed to finally blow all the candles out with a little help from Harry.

Pete went over to the stereo system by the far wall and put on a CD. The big band sounds of Glenn Miller came through the speakers and Dan swept Susie into his arms for a dance, Pete gently took his mother in his arms and they swayed to the music. "Ooh, this takes me back to the days when your dad and I danced all evening," Pearl said, gazing up at her son. "Your dad was a good dancer and he had all the moves. Do you remember when he was on the dance floor all the time?"

"Yep, I remember him twisting away in the sixties – so embarrassing!" Pete laughed.

"I'm not sure about any jiving though – I'll sit that one out and leave it to you young ones," Pearl joked.

They both laughed and Pete assured her he wasn't about to start throwing himself around either. He led his mother back to her seat and then gallantly held Ruby for a few minutes, dancing until she collapsed exhausted into the chair next to Pearl.

"So," said Ruby, "how is your birthday going? Are you having a nice time? Tony and Jeannie and Jack and Maria and their families send their love. They would have come along but I asked them not to as I wanted to have a bit of time with you on my own after the party. Jeannie is lovely but she can fuss about me sometimes – I hope you don't mind?" she rushed into the next sentence without hardly catching her breath – "I'm so sorry I haven't been in touch before, Pearl. I know you have written to me; Tony has passed the letters on to me from my old house. I honestly did mean to write back but, well, to be honest I haven't been myself for some time."

Pearl listened intently, all the while searching her friend's face for the real problem lurking below the surface chatter. Her face was as lined and wrinkled as Pearl's now, her chestnut hair was cut much shorter these days and was streaked through with grey; it actually suited her, and Pearl chided herself for still being envious of Ruby's hair after all these years.

"I'm having a lovely day and all the better for seeing you, my dear, it's a lovely surprise," she said. "How did you get here and how long are you staying?"

Ruby visibly relaxed even though Pearl was still staring at her. "My Tony organised a taxi to drop me off and the staff here have been talking to my lot at High End Home, where I moved to and I'm staying overnight until tomorrow afternoon, so we can have a good catch up later – if you would like to?" she asked nervously.

"Excellent! It's been far too long since we spent some time together. I thought I had upset you in some way, but no matter, you're here now and that's all that counts," said Pearl wondering what was really on Ruby's mind. "I didn't realise you had moved into a home too, is your one nice? How long have you been there? This one is marvellous and I'm so glad I made the move now, although it was difficult after Edward and I had lived for so long in our lovely home." Pearl realised she was wittering on, but she was becoming a bit unsettled by Ruby's obvious discomfort. She was about to ask her another question when her daughter approached.

"Here you are, you two, I've just cut you a small slice each for now, but there is plenty left." Susie handed them a plate each of birthday cake. "You look like you are having a good natter, was it a nice surprise to see Ruby, Mum?" she asked smiling.

"Oh, the best!" said Pearl. "I suppose you were all in on it?"

"Ha, ha! Yes," said Susie, laughing "it took a bit of organisation, but it was worth it to give you a lovely day – you have enjoyed it, haven't you?" she added a bit nervously, knowing her mother hated too much fuss.

"Yes, darling, it was lovely, you shouldn't really bother too much as I know you all have such busy lives, but it is appreciated so thank you all." Pearl was overcome with emotion and fumbled about for her hanky so Susie couldn't see her eyes welling up.

Susie handed out cake to the other residents and Ted smiled at her as she passed him the plate. "Lovely, thank you very much, girly, that looks just the job. I can't eat the little hard bits of icing though, they bugger up my plate you see, but I'll just leave them on the side!"

Susie smiled and left as soon as she could – in case he took his false teeth out to show her!

She made her way over to Hilda and offered her some cake, "Ooh, no, thank you, dear, I can't eat all that sweet stuff, it plays havoc with my innards! Did I tell you what the doctor said the last time he took a stool sample?" Hilda was always keen to let everyone know about her bowels and the problems she had with them.

"Er. Oh, yes, you mentioned it the last time I came in to see Mum. I'd love to stay and chat, Hilda, but I'd better get on with handing round the cake, I'll see you in a little while." Susie made her escape, next going over to Arthur who she knew was hard of hearing. If you spoke normally to him, he would tell you to speak up and if you shouted at him, he would get upset you were shouting at him – you couldn't win!

"Hello, Arthur, I've brought you some cake," Susie tried.

"BAKE? I DON'T BAKE! I'M IN A HOME YOU KNOW. THEY HAVE COOKS AND WHATNOT FOR ALL THAT!" Arthur barked back at her.

"I'VE BROUGHT YOU SOME CAKE!" Susie said louder.

"Cake, you say. Well, why didn't you say that, then? Silly girl, asking me if I bake!" he said.

"SO, WOULD YOU LIKE A SLICE?" Susie felt like a schoolgirl in front of the headmaster. She knew it was difficult, but she gritted her teeth and waited.

"NICE? Yes, it's supposed to be nice later, the weather is warm, and it is nearly summer, you know. Now, is there any of that lovely cake left?" Arthur looked about as everyone was tucking in.

Susie handed the plate to him and scuttled off back to Dan, who was watching her, smiling and trying not to laugh. "We'll all be like that one day, love," he said, putting his arm around her waist and kissing the top of her head.

"I know, it's just so hard to smile and not shove the cake in his face though! Yet, he is actually a really nice man. It must be so frustrating for him, even with his hearing aids in it must sound muffled, poor old chap," Susie said and stood with Dan watching the party and glad it was all going smoothly.

They had all taken lots of photos with their phones, but Simon had brought along his camera – he was a keen amateur photographer and was snapping away. He managed to get a particularly lovely one of Pearl and Ruby sitting together and decided to get it framed for them.

After some more modern dancing, and watching Harry wiggle about to the grown-ups' delight, the family started to make moves to leave about five thirty and everyone was waiting to hug and kiss Pearl and Ruby before they left, repeatedly saying their goodbyes then remembering some other snippet of news they'd forgotten to say earlier. It was close on six o'clock when eventually everyone had gone, and Pearl and Ruby sat quietly with the welcome cup of tea Jill had brought in.

"So, Ruby, are you going to tell me what's been happening and what is really troubling you?" Pearl asked her friend gently.

"Oh, Pearl, I have so much to tell you, but first I'm going to skip to the most important news and you definitely won't like it!" Ruby looked uncomfortable but determined as she looked at Pearl.

"I'm sure whatever you tell me won't shock me, dear," said Pearl. "Don't forget I've known you for the best part of eighty years, I think I can safely say I know you by now!" Pearl was chuckling now, assuming Ruby was going to tell her she'd met a man and was considering marriage – Ruby had had three weddings so far...

"Well, yes, you do know me very well, better than anyone I'd say, but, well, the thing is, er." Ruby suddenly was overcome with nerves despite her earlier convictions.

"Come on, spit it out, dear, you can tell me." She looked aghast at Ruby's face. "Whatever is it, Ruby?" said Pearl, feeling worried now.

"Right, well." Ruby took a deep breath and continued hurriedly, "Don't hate me, Pearl, but I'm booked to go away in three months' time."

"Ooh, lovely, a holiday! What will that be? The August Bank holiday weekend, isn't it?" Pearl cut in. "What an excellent idea, do you know I might come with you. I've been thinking a little trip to the coast might do me good, somewhere on the Suffolk coast might be an idea. What do you think? Where are you going? Not Spain or somewhere hot like that, are you? I can't stand the heat anymore and all those mosquitoes… Hang on, why on earth would I hate you for going on holiday? …, Ruby?"

"It's not a holiday exactly – well, it's not a holiday at all to be honest," said Ruby, taking a deep breath. "I'm going to Switzerland, Pearl, to a clinic there. It's Dignitas," she said as gently as she could. "I won't be coming back - well, not alive anyway!" Ruby gave a small gulp as she tried to make a joke and lighten Pearl's reaction.

Chapter 3
May 2018

Pearl slumped back into her chair feeling the shock course through her. She couldn't believe what Ruby had just said!

"I, I, don't understand, Ruby. Why? What has happened? Whatever it is I'm sure there's an alternative, you can't just take that kind of drastic move," Pearl said with desperation in her voice. "Let's talk this through later, don't make any rash decisions, dear."

"I've thought long and hard over this, Pearl. I know it sounds harsh, but I don't want to carry on like this anymore and I'm afraid nothing you or anyone else can say now will make me change my mind. My life isn't going to improve, so there is only going to be quantity and not quality for the time I have left. I want to go with my dignity intact and I absolutely dread becoming more of a burden than I already am."

Ruby tried to get Pearl to understand from her point of view. She had had the same conversation with her son Tony and his wife Jeannie. Her other son Jack and his wife Maria were equally upset, but eventually they had all accepted, albeit reluctantly, that it was her life and she should feel able to end it as she saw fit.

"Are you ill, is that it? Is it something terminal?" Pearl asked, reaching for her teacup and clinging onto it as if it was a lifeline while fearing the worst. Her hand was shaking, and she struggled to calm herself down.

"Well, yes, I am ill," Ruby began. "But it's not cancer or anything like that." She took a breath. "I have severe rheumatoid arthritis – as you can see – I have great difficulty getting up or sitting down. I can't manage without my bloody sticks! I can't stand for too long and stairs are nigh on impossible now. I have breathing problems – too many cigarettes all those years ago I expect – I also have a pacemaker as my poor old heart is on its last legs and the doctor diagnosed me with early onset dementia three months ago. Half of it is just age I know, but I do have problems remembering the names of things."

"Well, we are all getting a bit like that, Ruby," Pearl cut in again. "We can't be expected to remember everything, not at our age."

"I know some of it is just my age and I'm all right for now but none of it is going to go away, is it?" Ruby continued, "I'm not going to be skipping about and dancing the light fantastic ever again, am I? Like I said, I can't bear the thought of being stuck in a bed somewhere, helpless and not even knowing where I am, or who I am or who is looking after me."

She looked at Pearl, beseechingly willing her oldest friend to understand and be supportive. She knew it would take a while as Pearl was still looking white with the shock, but she hoped she would come around and see how determined Ruby was to go ahead with her plans.

"More tea, ladies?" said Jill brightly as she approached the two old friends with a tray ready to take their old tea things away. "Oh, my goodness!" she exclaimed as she suddenly saw Pearl's white face and shocked expression. "Pearl, are you okay? Whatever has happened? Are you feeling ill?"

Pearl stared at Jill with her mouth open as if she suddenly couldn't remember who she was. "Oh! Erm, hello, yes, I'm fine. I think it must just be all the excitement from the party – yes, that's it, just a bit overexcited!" Pearl blustered at last. She was still trying to take in Ruby's news and just couldn't get her head around it, as the young ones of today always say.

Jill looked from one to the other and could sense something wasn't quite right, but she could also see that neither of them was going to tell her what the problem was. "Maybe a light supper and an early night might be the best thing for you both after all that's been happening today?" Jill thought that Pearl definitely wasn't right, but she did have a bit of colour coming back to her face so maybe it wasn't anything too serious.

"Yes, I think that's an excellent idea," Ruby said, looking around for her sticks. "I could just about manage a sandwich or maybe a lightly boiled egg? I don't think I could eat too much after that delicious birthday cake!"

"I'll get the kitchen to prepare you both something. Would you like to eat in the dining room with the other residents or would you prefer to have it in your rooms?" Jill busied herself helping Pearl rise from the chair.

"I think, dear, I'd like to go to my room," Pearl said softly as she found her voice. "I think a bit of an early night might be best." She turned to Ruby, "I'll see you in the morning for breakfast, Ruby?" She watched as her friend shakily stood and gripped the sticks with her gnarled old hands, her face pinched with the pain and sudden tears welled up in her eyes.

"Yes, I think you're right, Pearl, an early night might do us both some good. It's been a lovely day but exhausting." Ruby slowly shuffled across the lounge floor and asked Jill if her room was ready and her bag unpacked. Jill assured her everything was ready. Michelle came in to assist her. Ruby looked back and said, "Goodnight, Pearl, see you in the morning."

"Is everything okay, Pearl?" asked Jill gently when it was just the two of them. She efficiently got Pearl ready and into her bed, plumping the pillows the way Pearl liked them.

"Yes, dear, Ruby just had some news I wasn't expecting, but it will be all right I'm sure. Don't worry about me, I'm fine honestly, just a bit tired I expect. I didn't sleep too well last night – all the excitement for today, I suppose!"

Pearl was anxious not to let Jill know what they had been talking about. She wasn't sure of the ramifications of telling the people who were trying to preserve your life and make it more comfortable for you that you were thinking of killing yourself! One thing she was certain of though was that they wouldn't be best pleased!

"Okay. Well, if you need anything in the night to help you sleep, just ring the bell. I think it's Janice on tonight so she will get you some tablets if you need any," Jill said, mentally making a note to speak to Janice and get her to pop in about ten o'clock and check to see if Pearl was all right.

Later, once Pearl was settled in her room and her half-eaten sandwich had been cleared away, she lay back against the pillows and thought about what Ruby had told her. After seeing the way Ruby had painfully tried to move and her obvious discomfort and embarrassment using her sticks, she was beginning to understand the reasons behind what Ruby planned to do. After all, in a way she had been kind of thinking along the same lines wishing she could be with her Edward again, hadn't she? But to make such a decision! Oh dear, what a mess, she thought. She closed her eyes and let her mind wander back to their younger days, to when she and Edward started out. Things were so much simpler when they didn't have a care in the world and their lives stretched out endlessly before them.

Chapter 4
June 1946

"Ah, Pearl, darling, you look utterly radiant!" Ruby stood with her hands on her hips, her peach bridesmaid dress fitting her perfectly and, with her small bouquet matching her dress, she was vision of loveliness. She was gazing at her dear friend as Pearl's mum adjusted her veil, repositioning the mother of pearl clip which held it in place.

"She looks wonderful, doesn't she?" Pearl's mum Gwen said, her hands shaking a bit with the emotion of it all. Pearl's mum and her aunts had made her dress and, while it was simple, they had sewn some lace over the bodice and added tiny seed pearls around the neckline.

"Is my lipstick smudged? Does it look all right?" Pearl peered at Ruby as her mum finished with the veil.

"Stop going on about your blooming lipstick will you!" Ruby said laughing at her friend's obsession with her lipstick. "It looks lovely, Janet has done a brilliant job with your hair and make-up – Edward will hardly recognise you!"

Janet from next door had come in early and helped Pearl, then dashed back home to get herself ready for the ceremony. Pearl's hair was elegantly waved and clipped back from her face and her eyes were cleverly shadowed to make the best of them and bring out the lovely blue in the irises.

"Come on you lot, time to go!" shouted Pearl's Uncle Jim from the hallway. He was driving her mum and Ruby to the church, then coming back for Pearl and her dad. He'd been up since dawn cleaning and polishing his second-hand Ford Prefect, Pearl's Auntie Ivy had tied some ribbon to the front, and it was gleaming.

"Now coming!" shouted back Ruby and Gwen in unison as they kissed Pearl good luck in a flurry of lace and perfume.

Silence! Pearl took a deep breath and checked herself in the mirror, her heart-shaped face was glowing – they were right, Janet had made her look like a movie star. She wasn't sure how Edward would feel seeing her all done up like this!

She was feeling strangely calm about the wedding, almost as if it was happening to someone else, but she was sure the nerves would kick in when she was walking down the aisle.

"Are you ready, love?" her dad John said softly knocking on the door.

"Yes, Dad, you can come in." she said, smoothing down the front of her dress.

"Oh, my beauty," John said his voice cracking. "You look beautiful, darling." He coughed, clearing his throat full of emotion and said, "Righto, we better get going, Jim's outside with the engine running. You don't want to be too fashionably late!"

Pearl collected her bouquet of freesias and carnations from the hall table and they were off!

The wedding passed in a blur of happiness, Edward beaming as she came slowly down the aisle towards him with tears in his eyes, the exchanging of vows and rings, then off to the reception. Everyone was dancing and having a good time and before she knew it, they were off on their honeymoon.

Edward had booked them three nights at a bed and breakfast in Great Yarmouth and the weather was supposed to be warm and dry. She was looking forward to spending a few days alone with Edward until they moved into the top two rooms at Edward's mother's house; it was only for a few months, Edward had explained, just until the little two up two down house which went with his job (Edward worked for the railway and was entitled to a tied cottage once he was married) became available.

Edward had lived alone with his elderly mother Eleanor, his father having passed away several years earlier and, although Pearl and Eleanor liked one another, Pearl was always a little worried how Eleanor would be once they had left, and she would be on her own.

Eleanor, however, was delighted for them and she said it had given her the push she needed to get out and meet some new friends, so everything was working out perfectly. She had also said she was looking forward to having grandchildren enormously and would they please hurry up and make her wish come true!

They had a lovely few days away and Eleanor took great delight in spoiling them for the time they were with her. All too soon their house was ready for them.

Their moving day finally came, and Pearl was so excited to be in her own home together with Edward. On the first floor they had one decent sized bedroom for themselves, a tiny second bedroom and a bathroom with a sink and a bath – the toilet was outside along the garden path – and downstairs was a good-sized kitchen with a larder. There was a small scullery outside the back door for washing and storage, and a small living room with a coal fire.

Once everything was finally in and put away, they collapsed on the small sofa with a celebratory sherry. Edward put his arm around Pearl and toasted their new beginnings. "Well, Mrs Turner, may we always be this happy and in love until we grow old."

"Cheers!" They both chinked their glasses together and sat enjoying their togetherness.

Edward looked at Pearl and knew he had made the very best decision of his life the day he had screwed up his courage and bought her a drink at the dance. "Now then, Mrs Turner," he said with a cheeky grin, "Are you very tired or should we try and fulfil my old mother's wishes?" Pearl giggled and they went upstairs, taking the sherry with them!

Chapter 5
May 2018

Pearl woke in the morning with a sense of foreboding and for a few moments couldn't work out what was wrong, then it all came flooding back to her. Ruby's announcement the night before had shocked her to her core. She wasn't sure what she would say to her when they came face to face at breakfast.

Oh, you're awake," said Jill as she came in with the fresh towels for the bathroom, "I'll just put these away then we'll get you up and about."

"Is Ruby up yet, dear?" asked Pearl hesitantly.

"Yes, she's having a cup of tea and chatting to the others in the breakfast room and waiting for you," Jill said, glancing back from the bathroom. "Are you all right, Pearl? You still look a bit pale. Did you sleep all right in the end after all the excitement from your party?"

"Yes, once I got off, I slept all right, I think that was it, just the excitement." Pearl was reluctant to say any more in case she ended up spilling it all out to Jill. They had bonded almost immediately Pearl had moved in and she felt awful deceiving Jill, she was almost like another daughter or granddaughter to her, but she couldn't say anything yet and, to be honest, it wasn't really her story to tell.

Ruby looked up as Pearl entered the breakfast room. "Hello, love," she said softly as Pearl took her seat beside her.

Before Pearl could answer, Ted shouted out, "Good morning, Pearl, sleep well? You're looking lovely as always!"

Ted, at eighty-three, still persisted in trying to woo Pearl, saying he could be her toy-boy any time she wanted! He raised his teacup in a salute and winked at her as best as he could with his rheumy old eyes.

"Good morning, everyone," Pearl said, glad for once of Ted's intervention so she was able to address the whole table rather than individually and avoid looking directly at Ruby. She had a horror of blurting out Ruby's news to everyone!

"Here you are, Pearl, a nice cup of tea and a slice of wholemeal toast for you." Michelle put the toast in front of Pearl. "Do you want some honey on it this morning?"

"Bugger the honey, she's sweet enough already!" Ted said chuckling.

Pearl laughed along with everyone else as she replied to Michelle, "No, I'm fine thank you, dear, I'll just have the toast today."

Gradually the others left to go to the television room and catch up on the news or go out for a walk round the grounds until their visitors arrived until just Pearl and Ruby were left sitting at the table.

"Please don't hate me," Ruby said struggling to hold back her tears as her luminous brown eyes brimmed over.

"Oh, sweetheart, I don't hate you, I could never hate you, you know that," Pearl's heart was breaking. "I've been thinking over what you were saying yesterday and, to be honest, I do sympathise and a part of me is envious of you."

"Envious? Of me?" Ruby wasn't expecting that.

"Well, I think it's a very brave decision to make and you've made it and come to terms with your own demise and you're dealing with it with dignity – which I suppose is the whole point really, isn't it?" Pearl said with compassion. "Tell me more about it and how you convinced your family etc. that that was what you wanted?"

For the next hour and a half Ruby filled Pearl in on all the decision making she had done; the research into the Swiss clinic and the procedures and tests she would have to undertake to ensure she had her wishes met fully and to be given the appropriate approvals necessary.

"Well, you have certainly done your research, Ruby," said Pearl later. They had moved into the lounge and were sitting side by side on the sofa. Pearl was amazed at all the detail and decision-making that had led Ruby to today.

"The hardest part was telling the boys. Tony and Jack wouldn't speak to me for weeks after I had told them what I was thinking of doing, but eventually, and with Jeannie and Maria's backing, they were willing to listen and now they have accepted that, ultimately, it's my decision." Ruby looked slightly more relaxed now she had finally told Pearl what was going on – she had hated not telling her before, but she was determined to get it all organised first.

"So, has this taken you eight years then?" Pearl asked curiously. She had written to Ruby several times over the last few years but, apart from birthday and Christmas cards and the odd postcard now and then, Ruby had not replied in any great detail.

Pearl had thought she had upset Ruby in some way and wanted to reach out to her. Their children had tried to get them together over the years but, for various reasons, the time had got away from them and it was almost eight years since they last spent time with each other.

"Erm – no, not for the whole time," Ruby looked at Pearl grinning sheepishly. "I got married – again!"

"Aha! I thought it might have something to do with a man!" Pearl was relieved to hear it wasn't anything she had done. She was well used to Ruby's track record with her husbands.

She had married Jim Sewell first and they had seemed to be happy, but after a few years he had left the scene. It turned out he had another life fifty miles away with another 'wife' and children. Jim had the ideal job as a travelling salesman and Ruby didn't suspect anything at first. When she eventually did find out, it was the typical clichéd suspicion – she found a note in one of his pockets. The marriage had been annulled with Ruby thanking her lucky stars they had no children together; she had been heartbroken and swore herself off men forever. Eighteen months later, she was engaged to Derek Clancy! A friend of hers had followed him surreptitiously for weeks after he had asked her to go out and finally convinced her that he lived with his parents and, as far as he could tell, certainly didn't have any children. They were married six months later.

They were happily married and lived with their sons Anthony and Jack until Derek's sudden death from a heart attack. They had thirty-five blissful years together and Ruby was heartbroken to lose him.

Ruby was alone for a few years as her sons were both married and had left home, then she had met Colin Hughes on a night out with Pearl and Edward. He worked with Edward and he had come along as his wife had died several months before and he had hardly left the house. Ruby and Colin hit it off and after a brief courtship they married in the local register office, Pearl and Edward were their witnesses, and they seemed happy together.

The last time Pearl had seen Ruby properly was at Colin's funeral ten years ago. They had had a brief get together at a party for one of the grandchildren two or three years later, but Pearl had taken ill and gone home early.

"So, after Colin had passed away, I thought you were going to grow old gracefully?" Pearl said wryly, waiting for Ruby's reaction. "What's your surname now, then? I've been sending the letters and cards to 'Ruby Hughes'."

"So, did I!" said Ruby, "but you know me, I just don't do very well on my own. I seem to need having a man around – oh, not for sex, that's no longer important, but just for the companionship, you know? My surname is Jenkins now, and that's the last man's name I will ever take!" she said emphatically.

"Yes, I know exactly what you mean, I get lonely too even though there are people around me all day long. I miss Edward dreadfully, but I could never replace him, so I've never been interested in anyone else." Pearl said wistfully, her mind full of Edward's voice and his lovely smile which always lit up when she walked in the room.

"You see, that's the thing, with you and Edward it was true love, that once in a lifetime love that most people never experience. I suppose that's what I've been looking for but never seem to find. I think it's the real thing and then a few years later it all falls apart," Ruby said sadly. "Apart from Derek, of course, he was truly a wonderful man and I wanted for nothing while he was alive."

"Yes, Derek was a lovely man and he adored you. You have to work at it though, dear, it doesn't always run smoothly. Me and Edward had some rows but the making up was always worth it!" Pearl winked at Ruby. "So, what happened this time?"

"Well, after Jim left and Derek and Colin passed away, I thought I would be on my own. Then two years after Colin I met Mike at bingo; he was younger than me which I thought was a good thing. All these husbands passing away, I was expecting a knock at the door from the police with a search warrant looking for poison! He was fun and seemed genuinely interested in me." Ruby tailed off bewilderment in her eyes.

"How much younger?" Pearl asked suspiciously.

"Oh, not too young, only thirteen years, so he was sixty-six when I first met him. He'd just retired and was looking for the same as me – companionship – or so I thought. We seemed to hit it off and started spending more time together, then it slowly dawned on me that every time we went anywhere, he had conveniently left his wallet behind or forgotten his credit card." Ruby looked at Pearl's expression which was one of exasperation.

"So, he was fleecing you blind?" said Pearl. "How much for?"

"Well, over the seven-year period we were together, it worked out about fifteen thousand pounds." Ruby now couldn't look at Pearl, she felt like a naughty schoolgirl, "Don't look so disapproving, Pearl, I was so ashamed you can't make me feel any worse!"

"Oh, my god!" Pearl gasped clutched her throat. "Fifteen thousand pounds! How could you let it go on so long? Have you managed to get any of it back?"

"It didn't seem to be too much at the time, you know, a few pounds here and there. Then he needed some money immediately to buy a car and he said he was waiting for some sort of bonus thing to come through from a pension and – Oh, I don't know, Pearl, he sounded so plausible and I was so gullible, it still makes me feel sick to think of it, but yes I've got it all back.

"Tony and Jack and a few of their friends went and 'had a word' with him. I don't know all the details and I'm not sure I do want to know, but a couple of months later I got a cheque for the fifteen thousand. I don't know why he did it if he obviously had the money – unless he borrowed it from someone else. I don't know, anyway, we were divorced quietly a year ago and I haven't seen or heard from him since."

Ruby had been so upset by it all she'd kept away from all her friends and it was only Tony, Jack and their wives who knew anything about it. She had wanted to speak to Pearl about it before now, but her health had started to deteriorate and her plans for the clinic had come to fruition, so really now was the perfect timing.

"Well, that's something, I suppose." Pearl patted Ruby's hand reassuringly. "And this is how you're funding…" She tailed off as she spotted Jill approaching.

"Hello, ladies, are you ready for your lunch?" Jill looked closely at Pearl who seemed to be in much better form today. "We have chicken soup and sausage and mash for lunch and, if you can eat any more after that, there's a bit of your birthday cake left, Pearl."

After lunch they chatted some more before Ruby's transport arrived to take her back to her home. "So, you see," said Ruby, picking up the tale again, "Once I had the lump sum back it all seemed to slot into place. I could actually do what I planned and in a way Mike did me a favour as I don't think I would have been able to save the whole fifteen thousand and, even if I was able to, it would have probably taken me a lot longer and it got me thinking this is my chance to carry out my wishes while I could. I've paid for the flights and accommodation for Tony, Jack and their wives. They didn't want me to, but I insisted if they were coming with me, I would pay for it and there's still some left over for the family to share."

"Well, yes, I do see how it was fortuitous in the end, and I can absolutely see what you're planning makes sense, none of us want to be a burden as we get older, but it still seems extreme, my dear, so many people are going to miss you but no one more than me," Pearl said, the tears threatening to spill over again.

"But that's the whole point, Pearl, I'll miss you too, of course I will, but if I was still here and couldn't recognise you or my lads, or indeed anyone else I know, surely that's the greater loss for everyone? Far better that I am able to say goodbye to the people I love while I still know who they are and they will remember me as a whole person, not just a shell and a shadow of who I once was, if that makes any sense?"

"Yes, it makes perfect sense." Pearl was openly crying now. "I suppose in a way it's what we all want, isn't it? After all, we are all going to die eventually so why not make it as painless as possible?"

"Exactly!" Ruby was smiling through her tears. "I'm so glad you can understand me, Pearl. Believe me, this hasn't been an easy decision to make and I've spent many a long night wondering if I should do this or not, but at the end of the day the same answers come back to me. I really won't improve, and things will only go downhill – well, more downhill than they already are at any rate!"

The car pulled up and Michelle came out to help the driver get Ruby comfortable in the back seat. The two friends had reluctantly broken their embrace and were waving to one another, promising to see each other before Ruby left the country for good.

After Ruby had gone and Pearl had waved until she could no longer see the car, she made her way back into the lounge area and sat in her favourite seat. Jill kindly brought her a cup of tea and a couple of biscuits, but she didn't ask Pearl anything about Ruby's visit. She knew Pearl would talk to her if she needed to and, as Pearl wasn't looking so shell shocked, she was happy Pearl was all right.

Pearl sat sipping her tea, thinking what a strange couple of days it had been. Her birthday party was wonderful, and it was so lovely to see the family and she was so grateful they took the time to visit and she had received some lovely gifts. Then Ruby's announcement had thrown her completely. It was obvious Ruby had given it a great deal of thought and now she had the backing of her sons and their wives, she could see what Ruby was saying was right; it was far better to go with dignity than lying in a bed somewhere not knowing who you were or anything. She gave a little shudder as the thought occurred to her that was exactly how she could become, and not in the too distant future either.

She knew she would have to discuss it with someone and resolved to have a chat to Susie when she next popped in on Tuesday. With that decision made, her eyes fluttered, and she drifted off to sleep.

Chapter 6
July 1947

"Yoo hoo. Pearl, are you up?"

It was Sunday morning and Pearl and Edward were having a bit of a lie in, hoping their hangovers would be gone soon; they had been out the night before celebrating their first wedding anniversary. When Pearl heard Ruby's voice and a knocking on the front door, Edward reached across for the alarm clock and said, "It's half past eight for goodness sake! What on earth does she want at this hour?"

"You know Ruby, it could be anything!" Pearl said, pulling on her candlewick dressing gown and trying to make herself look presentable. "Where's my handbag? I can't find my lipstick!"

"It's in the living room, love," said Edward chuckling. "Don't you remember? You dropped it on the floor when we got in last night from the pub; you were a little bit tipsy! What on earth do you need your lipstick for? It's only Ruby!"

Pearl gave him a withering look. "I can't open the door without my lipstick in place, it just wouldn't be right!" She made her way down the stairs and saw her handbag by the sofa. She quickly gave her lips a quick slick and went to the front door.

Ruby was hopping up and down on the doorstep eagerly waiting for Pearl to open the door.

"Ooh, there you are, let me in quick!" Ruby said excitedly as Pearl finally managed to get the door open after wrestling with the lock which always seem to stick.

"You'll have to have a look at that lock, Edward, when you have a minute," Pearl shouted up to Edward who had just gone into the bathroom.

"Will do," came the muffled reply.

"Never mind about the lock, have a look at this!" Ruby flashed her left hand in front of Pearl's face. There sitting on her third finger was a solitaire diamond ring; Ruby's cheeks were glowing, and her eyes were alight with love. "Jim proposed last night; went down on one knee and everything!"

"Oh, my goodness, that is beautiful, congratulations, sweetheart!" Pearl was excited for her friend but, to be honest, she had never really taken to Jim. On the few occasions they had met there seemed to be something just not right. She hadn't been able to put her finger on what it was, but Edward had said something similar, so she knew it wasn't just her. Still, her best friend was engaged, and she was truly happy for her.

"Do I hear congratulations are in order?" Edward appeared in the doorway with a bottle of champagne and some glasses. The champagne was a gift from his mother for their anniversary, but they were too tipsy the night before to open it.

He glanced over at Pearl and she imperceptibly shook her head silently saying, 'not now we'll talk about it later'.

"Ooh, Edward it's a bit early for champers, isn't it?" Ruby said, grabbing one of the glasses in readiness.

"Never too early in my book for champagne," said Edward, thinking a hair of the dog might help his headache. He deftly released the cork with a pop and a flourish, and they all laughed as the bubbles rose out of the top of the bottle.

"Quick, catch it, Pearl, don't want to waste any!" Edward gave Pearl her glass and they toasted Ruby's good news. "Where is Jim then?" Edward looked to the door as if Jim was about to walk in. "Shall I get another glass if he's on his way?"

"Ah, yes Jim, erm… he's not coming, he has an important client to see today so he was up and out by seven this morning," Ruby said apologetically. "He won't be back until tomorrow."

"A client? On a Sunday?" Edward was regarding Ruby while also glancing across to Pearl who had sat down at the dining table.

"Well, yes, apparently this bloke owns his own company and he is very busy during the week so the only time he could fit Jim in was this morning. It's a deal worth quite a bit of money and Jim says if he lands it, it will near enough pay for the wedding!"

"So, have you set a date yet?" Pearl asked keen to move on before Edward started asking too many awkward questions.

"I wanted to get married at Christmas, but Jim thinks we should get hitched sooner so it might be in September now, towards the end of the month." Ruby was so excited she didn't notice the glances back and forth between Pearl and Edward.

"Well, that doesn't give you long to get everything organised as it's nearly the end of July now." Pearl was wondering what the rush was. Ruby hadn't said anything about having children so as far as she knew she wasn't pregnant.

"It will just be a register office wedding, Jim's not a church person, so there shouldn't be too much to do and organise," Ruby said with a hint of wistfulness as if she would prefer her wedding to be a bit more glamorous. "We are going to have afternoon tea at the Lamb Inn afterwards if they can fit us in. Will you come with me next week to look at wedding dresses, Pearl? Oh, and would you both please be our witnesses?" Ruby was quite breathless by the time she had finished.

"We would love to and I'm sure Pearl will only be so happy to go shopping." Edward was grinning and hugging first Pearl then Ruby as he had decided whatever he and Pearl thought, it was Ruby's day and they would support her.

"Yes, yes, of course," Pearl said. She still couldn't shake off the feeling that something wasn't quite right, but she knew Ruby would confide her in later if she wanted to.

"Oh, I'm so pleased, thank you," Ruby was smiling and laughing now. "I wasn't sure how you were going to take the news as its short notice. Now, is there any more champagne left, I love the bubbles?"

"I think there's a drop left." Edward drained the last of the bottle into their glasses. "To marriage!" he toasted.

The wedding indeed took place at the end of September. Jim's family were conspicuous by their absence; neither his parents nor any siblings had turned up for the day. He was rather off hand about it all, saying they didn't really get along and weren't a close family, so there was just a small crowd for the afternoon reception tea with Pearl's parents helping to make up the numbers.

Three years later Ruby discovered he was living a double life with another 'wife' and children fifty miles away. Jim was arrested for bigamy and their marriage was annulled. Pearl was a tremendous support for Ruby, despite the urge to say, 'I told you so', and everyone including Ruby was just grateful that they hadn't had any children together.

Chapter 7
May 2018

Pearl had slept surprisingly well that night even after her afternoon nap and Jill was relieved to see she had some colour back in her face when she was up and about. Pearl had come to a decision and once she had spoken to Susie, she hoped the burden of guilt would disappear. She spent the day chatting with Ted who was highly delighted and was even more ardent to gain her affections. "So, Pearl, would you like to help me to finish this blasted jigsaw puzzle? There are a few bits left and I'm buggered if I can see where they go!" Ted asked, hoping Pearl would stay in the lounge for a bit longer with him.

"I'll have a look," she replied, "but my eyes aren't so good in this light. How much have you got left to do?"

They spent another hour fiddling about with the pieces until Pearl cried off with an impending headache. "I'm going to have a little lie down now I think, Ted. Thank you for this morning, it was fun."

"The pleasure's all mine," Ted said, beaming and grimacing at the same time as he tried to gallantly stand as Pearl was leaving.

"Don't get up, you silly old fool, stay there and finish your puzzle." Pearl gave him a wave and went to her room, slightly concerned that she had encouraged Ted a little too much.

After dinner the residents were treated to a play put on by the local amateur dramatic society – *Rebecca* by Daphne du Maurier. It was one of Pearl's favourites and she thoroughly enjoyed it.

They all enjoyed hot chocolate and biscuits while they sat and discussed the evening and before long Pearl's eyelids were closing of their own accord and she managed to catch Jill's eye before she nodded off completely. "I'm ready for my bed now," Pearl said contentedly, all thoughts of Ruby put to one side for now.

The following morning Pearl was eagerly awaiting Susie's arrival. She had said she would be there by eleven o'clock and it was now coming up to a quarter to so she wouldn't have long to wait. She eventually saw Susie's car pull into the car park and was glad she was a bit early. As Susie came through into the hall Pearl could see she was talking to Jill; she guessed they were discussing her strange behaviour on the day of the party. Ah well, Susie would find out everything within the next half hour or so.

They sat outside on the patio and after Michelle had bought their tea they sipped in silence for a few minutes.

"So, Mum, how have you been since Saturday?" Susie started the conversation. She had indeed had a word with Jill who had told her how worried she had been during Ruby's visit, but that she had seemed to brighten up and hadn't said anything about what was obviously troubling her.

"I'm fine, darling, thank you for all the trouble you went to. It was a wonderful day and it was lovely to see Ruby again after all these years, so well done!" Pearl realised she was blustering, and she suddenly thought how on earth can I tell my own daughter something like this?

Of course, Susie and Pete had known Ruby and Derek since they were born, just as Tony and Jack had known Pearl and Edward. They had all lived their lives so closely.

Susie and Pete were three years older than Tony and Jack was the youngest coming along two years later, so they had all grown up together and had many of the same friends from their childhoods. They had shared birthday parties and gone on holidays with each other's families several times.

"Yes, Tony initially contacted me, and I've been phoning him for the last few weeks and getting everything organised for Ruby to stay over etc. Pete and I organised the cake from Shepherds – I wasn't going to try and make one for such a special occasion! Jill has been in on it too as she was the link between Jane at High End and Margaret here, but it all worked out beautifully in the end, so it was worth it," Susie said.

"It's just such a pity Ruby probably won't be getting all that for her own ninetieth birthday, isn't it?" Pearl said softly almost to herself.

"What on earth do you mean, Mum?" Susie was now looking strangely at her mother. "Why won't Ruby get a birthday party? I'm sure Tony and Jack will want to celebrate it with her. I know they couldn't make it to yours but apparently Ruby had said she wanted to see you on her own first as it had been such a long time since you had seen each other – Mum, what's going on? What do you know?"

"Oh, my darling, it's not really my story to tell but if Tony and Jack haven't said anything to you and Pete then I'd better let you know exactly what Ruby is up to." Pearl gripped Susie's hand and started to relate all that Ruby had told her over the weekend.

"Oh, my god! No! I don't believe it!" Susie was horrified once Pearl had told her everything,

"I can't believe Tony didn't say anything – all those phone calls and he never said a word. Well, he could have told me she was planning on telling you something like this – at your own birthday party too!" Susie was indignant and angry. "Just wait until I get home and I'll give him a piece of my mind! Have you said anything to Pete?"

"No, dear, I haven't spoken to anyone else about it as I wanted to talk to you first. I completely understand your reaction, in fact I was pretty much the same, I just couldn't believe what she was telling me," Pearl continued. "But when I had calmed down a bit – as you will too, darling – it started to make sense and I can completely understand her decision. The thing is, Susie, as much as we are upset by it all, it comes down to what Ruby feels is best for her doesn't it? … and Susie please don't be upset by this, but…" Pearl took a deep breath before she could continue, "I'm going with her."

Susie's reaction was the complete opposite to Pearl's amazement; she'd gone from being angry and almost apoplectic to suddenly diminishing in front of Pearl's eyes.

"But why, Mum? Why on earth would you plan something like this without telling me or Pete? Did Ruby put you up to it?" Susie was sniffling into her tissue and trying to keep her emotions in check. "You're not ill or anything are you? I'm sure Jill would have said something. You haven't had to have the doctor out, have you?"

"Sorry, my darling, that came out all wrong. I meant I want to go with Ruby to Switzerland just to be with her, you know, at the end. I didn't mean that I wanted to go the same way!" Pearl was mortified now and instead of feeling better about telling Susie she now felt even worse! "If I was planning anything like that don't you think I would talk to you and Pete about it first? I'm hoping when it's my time I'll just go quietly in my sleep."

Susie was gripping Pearl's hand so tightly Pearl was sure she would end up with a bruise.

"Oh, Mum!" Susie was openly crying now, luckily releasing Pearl's hand to get more tissues from her bag. "I can't imagine how you must have been feeling these last few days, you should have rung me earlier and I would have come over straightaway."

"I did consider it, darling, but I needed time to process the information myself and I do feel better for speaking to you about it now, but please don't get angry with Tony and Jack. I think they have all come to terms with their mum's decision now and Ruby wanted to tell me before anyone else outside of their family." Pearl was now holding Susie's hand hoping to instil some understanding that it was the best thing for Ruby.

"So," Susie breathed in deeply, "Let me get this straight, you just want to go with Ruby for company and you have no plans to contact Dignitas yourself?"

"No, dear, of course not. If I'm honest I have been thinking a lot about Dad lately and how much I miss him, but I know we will be together again when the time comes so I'm happy to wait until that day." Pearl's eyes were shining with tears as Susie hugged her with relief.

"Well! What a morning, I certainly wasn't expecting anything like this!" Susie smiled weakly at Pearl, her cheeks flushed, and her beautiful blue eyes clouded with more unshed tears. "I'm not sure what to do next, Mum. Do you think I should contact Tony and Jack, or will Ruby have told them now that you know what's happening and they might ring me or Pete?"

"Hmm, I'm really not sure the best way to go about it, I hadn't thought much beyond telling you," Pearl said thoughtfully. "I suppose you could invite them all over for drinks or something with Pete of course and then broach the subject? But I wouldn't tell any of the grandchildren anything, that's something that can be discussed later."

"Yes, that's a good idea. I'll talk to Dan tonight; he will be devastated I know. He's very fond of Ruby and will be heartbroken to hear this. Are you going to be all right, Mum? I can stay the rest of the day if you want?" Susie had some errands to do and she was going to pop into Milly's and take Harry to the park for an hour so she could put her feet up, but all that could wait if her mum needed her.

"No, dear, I'm fine, really. You get off and spend some time with little Harry, he'll be looking forward to having a go on the swings I expect." Pearl was feeling exhausted and emotional in equal measure.

"Okay, well, if you're sure?" Susie reluctantly got up to go. "I'll speak to Dan and Pete tonight and I'll come back in on Thursday to give you an update and see how you are. I love you, Mum," she said, the tears threatening again and hugged her goodbye. "Do you want to go inside now, or shall I ask Jill or Michelle to bring you another cup of tea?"

"I think I'll sit out here a bit longer, dear; the sun is lovely and warm and if I go in Ted will want me to help him again with his wretched puzzle! Would you ask the girls if I can have some more tea and could they bring my other cardigan, just in case the sun goes in?" Pearl wanted to be alone with her thoughts for a while longer.

"Of course, I will." Susie was more cheerful now, especially now she knew her mother wasn't planning anything drastic!

Michelle came out after ten minutes or so with a fresh pot of tea and Pearl's blue cashmere cardigan. "Here you are, my lovely," she said. "This will keep the chill off while you're out here. I'll pour your tea for you and come back in about twenty minutes to see if you are ready to go in."

"Thank you so much, dear." Pearl settled back in her chair with a cushion behind her and the cardigan across her shoulders, she lifted her face up to the sun and savoured the warmth on her closed eyes.

She imagined she could see Edward's smiling face looking down on her from above and she spoke to him softly, '*Oh, my darling, I do miss you and if you see him would you ask Derek if he thinks Ruby is doing the right thing? I'm so worried about her.*'

Chapter 8
May 2018

Susie had called Pete on her way to Milly's and invited him to dinner with her and Dan. She hadn't wanted to say too much over the phone although she reassured him that their mum was fine, but she'd heard some news about Ruby and wanted to chat with him about it.

She spent the afternoon with Milly and took Harry to the park and was glad of the distraction. Her mind was overloaded with thoughts of Ruby and her mother and the short break did her good. She had a quick coffee with Caroline to discuss Milly's impending stay in hospital and looking after Harry but didn't say anything to her about Ruby.

Soon she was back home to the lovely old house she and Dan had bought when they first got married. She had loved it on first sight and still felt its warmth enveloping her every time she came in. The large garden had been the bonus as it was perfectly secluded, and the children had played happily out there for years in the summer. As she was preparing the evening meal, she related her morning with Pearl to Dan.

"Bloody Hell!" said Dan in amazement, "I think we both need a drink after that news!" He selected a

Merlot from the wine rack, and as he poured them a generous glass of wine each he said, "So, when exactly is this all supposed to be happening? I assume Tony, Jack and their families will go with Ruby to Switzerland? Your mother certainly can't travel alone at her age, so are we all going to go as well? Sorry, darling, too many questions! I'm just trying to get my head around it all, you must have been devastated when your mum told you." He put his glass down and took Susie in his arms and hugged her.

Susie carefully put down the knife she'd been chopping carrots with and hugged him back. They had been through some testing times in their marriage, but she knew she could rely on Dan to support her. She thanked her lucky stars yet again for the day Dan Finch came into her life. It was at Pete and her joint eighteenth birthday party; he was a friend of Pete's from college and they had met up by chance and Pete had invited him along.

"Yes, it was a shock especially when Mum said she was going with Ruby! I thought I was going to faint clean away until she explained she just wanted to be there for Ruby at the end. Oh, Dan, what if Mum changes her mind and decides she wants to do it too?"

"Well, she said she didn't so let's not worry too much about that. What time is Pete arriving? I'll get the chops going now, shall I?" Dan had been thinking the same thing as Susie, but he could see how distraught she was.

"He'll be here in about half an hour, so we have plenty of time." Susie put the carrots on and started on the green beans.

Pete arrived just as the meal was being dished up. "Ah, that looks lovely, Susie. Hello, mate, how's things?" Pete gratefully accepted the glass of wine from Dan and took his place at the table. Pete had never married, preferring the bachelor lifestyle. He'd had several relationships, but they were never strong enough to make him want to take the final commitment.

"I'm good, thanks," Dan said, helping Susie serve the dinner.

"So, what's the old girl been up to now – not another bloody wedding, is it?" Pete said, chuckling, "No wonder I don't want to get married if Ruby and her trips to the aisle are any kind of gauge!" Pete waited until Susie had sat down and raised his glass for a toast. "Well, here's to a good Merlot and a lovely home cooked meal and you two!" They chinked glasses, and it was then Pete noticed his sister was quiet and hasn't replied to his comment about Ruby. "Sis, what's happened?" Pete put his glass down and looked from one to the other hoping someone would tell him what was going on.

Susie took a deep breath and then let it out as a sigh. The chops were going cold and congealing on their plates by the time she had told him everything. Dan had opened a second bottle in the meantime and kept topping up their glasses.

"Well, good on her, that's what I say!" Pete was full of admiration for Ruby at this stage. "I think it's brilliant! Well, not the fact that she's going to die obviously, but that she's able to decide how and when she goes!"

"Yes, I know what you mean, Pete." Susie was slowly coming around to the idea. "I'm just worried now how Mum is going to be afterwards."

"Hmm, yes it will be hard for her, I imagine, they have been friends – well, more like sisters really all these years. So, Tony and Jack haven't said anything to you?" Pete was surprised they had kept quiet and not mentioned it, although they hadn't been as close in recent years as they all were when they were younger. "Look, I'm playing golf with Tony tomorrow, I can have a word if you like? See how the land lies?"

"Yes, would you? We were thinking of having them over for drinks or something so we could all discuss it together, but I'm not sure how to approach them if they don't want to say anything." Susie and Dan started to clear the plates.

"Can I take mine home please, sis? It'll save me cooking something later!" Pete said. He usually just microwaved something, so he wasn't going to miss a dinner cooked for him. Susie carefully scraped it into a plastic tub for him to reheat later.

"So, you'll let me know what Tony says? I'm going to see Mum again in the next day or two so I can update her then."

"Yeah, sure. I'll give you call tomorrow night and let you know. What time are you going to Willow Lodge? I'll come with you if you like?" Pete wanted to see how his mum was coping with the news for himself.

"Oh, yes please, Pete, that will be great. I usually get there around eleven, once the breakfasts are out of the way and just before they get started on the lunches."

"Excellent! Now, are you in a rush for me to get off or is there another glass of that excellent Merlot going?" He winked at Dan who, grateful that his brother-in-law was on side, rooted about for another bottle. They moved to the living room and chatted about nothing in particular to try and alleviate the tension Susie was still feeling. They ended up having cheese and biscuits an hour later to soak up some of the wine and Pete called a taxi home as he certainly wasn't fit to drive! "I hope I'm okay for golf tomorrow," he said slurring his words a bit as he climbed into the back of the cab, "I can't let old Tony beat me!"

Chapter 9
May 2018

Ruby was feeling so much better now she had spoken to Pearl and 'cleared the air' so to speak. She had been feeling dreadful about not visiting her friend and was so ashamed of all the business with that toad Mike Jenkins, she should have known Pearl would always be on her side – even if she didn't always agree with her!

Tony had phoned to ask if it had gone okay and was it now okay to talk to Susie and Pete about her plans? He was playing golf with Pete and he didn't want it to be awkward, he explained. She gave him her blessing and hoped they wouldn't hate her. Over the last few months she had been back and forth with her decision-making until eventually she had come to realise this was the only decision for her.

She had talked to doctors and counsellors until she didn't think there was anyone left to talk to in the medical profession! Tony and Jack had taken her to Switzerland two months ago and she had been interviewed by the medical board. They had toured the clinic and facilities and the options available for the self-administering of drugs on the day. They had discussed what she wanted to happen to her afterwards;

the clinic had even asked if she wanted to listen to some music. She wasn't sure what would be appropriate and had finally settled on Vivaldi's *The Four Seasons,* one of her favourite classical pieces. She had started to believe it was all happening to someone else as it was all very matter of fact and emotionless, but she realised this was how they dealt with it.

Tony and Jack had had some uncomfortable moments listening to all the processes – Jack especially and several times he had had to leave the room – but she was so proud of the unwavering support from both her sons and she couldn't have loved them more.

She felt she had almost tied up all the loose ends of her life now; Pearl knew, her children were on side and all the arrangements had been made, she now had just three months left to live! Her friends – none as close as Pearl – obviously wouldn't be told anything other than she was going to Europe on a little holiday.

The retirement home had also been very supportive, providing counsellors and other experts on hand should she need them. Her GP continued to prescribe the medicines she required daily to function and would do so until the last day if required.

She knew Tony and Jack wanted to have a service for her back home afterwards so she had agreed and was trying to think of three pieces of music she wanted played; she didn't think *Chattanooga Choo, Choo* or *Pennsylvania 6-500* – both two of her favourite Glenn Miller songs – would be right, but then, people today had whatever they liked and meant something to them at their funerals, so she might just choose them!

She then started to think of all the inappropriate songs that could be played at funerals: *Stayin' Alive*; *Wish me luck as you wave me goodbye*; *Always look on the bright side*!

She started laughing out loud at that last one and found she couldn't stop, so much so that Mandy, who was just about to tell Ruby that afternoon tea was ready, asked her if she was all right and was there anything, she could do, or should she call the doctor? That made her laugh even harder and she was worried she was getting hysterical. Tears of laughter rolled down her face, her heart was pounding, and she couldn't breathe properly – after all this planning and expense she thought how typical it would be if she went right now. She eventually calmed down and Mandy brought her some water; she couldn't really tell Mandy what she was laughing about as she knew it would start her off again. She would have to try and remember to tell Tony and Jack and they could all have a chuckle together.

She sat in her room after tea, now writing letters to her great-grandchildren. It was taking her some time as her love for the children was sending more tears streaming down her cheeks unchecked. She thought she had spent most of the day in tears – Oh, the tears weren't for herself, they were for the hopes and dreams of the youngsters who had their whole lives still to look forward to.

She had written one to her grandchildren Tom, Jake, Kirsty and Maddie. They were not going to be told the real reason for her visit to Switzerland, but she had written a joint letter to them declaring her love and wishing them well in their lives and to be given to them after she had gone. There would be a small sum of money bestowed on each of them which Tony would provide them with as he was the executor of the estate – not that she had much of an estate!

Tom was Tony and Jeannie's eldest son, at forty-three he was the same age as Fleur. Tom was married to the lovely Karen; their son Oliver and his wife Megan were expecting their second baby in a few weeks.

Tony's other son Jake was three years younger and married to Claire. They had two children, but neither were married, both had good careers and had decided to wait until they were thirty before marrying and thinking about a family.

Kirsty and Maddie were Jack's lovely girls, both in their twenties. Neither was married, although Kirsty was engaged to Jordan who was a lovely young man and Maddie's boyfriend was Matt.

Ruby thought about Oliver and Megan's baby. She was due not long after Milly, she mused, how their lives were so interwoven since that first day at school all those years ago when Miss Masters had placed her next to Pearl.

Now here she was writing to her grandchildren and her great-grandchildren! She knew Tom and Karen were hoping for a little girl this time, their three-year-old grandson Will was hoping for a brother though.

She had a feeling if it was a girl, they might call her Ruby, which pleased her enormously. She sat back in her chair for a moment and thought back to when Pearl had told her she was finally expecting a baby, little did they know at the time it would be twins! Having twins was still a novelty in those days.

Chapter 10
August 1949

The day was blazing hot; it hadn't rained for days and everyone was wilting with the heat and humidity. Ruby and Pearl were having lunch in the Lyons tearooms in the city centre, their orders had just arrived and, as her plate was put in front of her, Pearl looked green around the gills. "You all right, Pearl? You look a bit pasty. It's a bit warm in here isn't it?" Ruby looked at her friend anxiously.

"Hmm… Oh, yes I'm okay, just not feeling too hungry all of a sudden." She sneaked a glance at the cod and chips on her plate and could feel her stomach rebelling at the thought of all the grease. "I think I must be coming down with something – I can't face it." She was terrified she was going to be sick and sipped some water with Ruby looking concerned for her.

"I'll get the waitress to take yours away, shall I?" Ruby looked longingly at her lunch, but she couldn't very well start munching in front of Pearl who was definitely not looking very well.

"Do you mind?" Pearl said. "I think I'm going to be sick!" She raced off to the toilets and Ruby quickly called over the waitress to remove the offending lunch.

Ruby picked half-heartedly at her cod, ate a few chips then, with a sigh, got up and went to the toilets in search of Pearl, who had been gone for several minutes now. She could hear her retching in the third stall along.

"Oh, my god, Pearl, are you, all right? Do you want me to come in?" She hovered outside the door. "Should I get the doctor? Pearl? Can you hear me?"

"I'll be out in a minute," came the weak reply. Pearl thought it must have been the cottage pie they had had for tea the other night, maybe the mince should have been used up sooner especially with the weather being as warm as it had been. The thought of the food set her off again and she was shaking by the time she managed to get the door open and all but fell into Ruby's arms.

"My goodness, you look dreadful. Do you think you can walk? I'll help you get home and then I'll call in to work for you and tell them you've been taken bad and probably won't be back in this afternoon and probably not tomorrow either." Ruby was thinking ahead quickly, if she could get Pearl home – and it wasn't too far – she could race over to the railway and see if Edward was about. He would know what to do. Jim was away working – as usual – so she couldn't rely on him to help out. If Edward could get home to be with Pearl, then Ruby would try and leave work early and pop in to see how she was. While she was still with Pearl, Edward could run to her mum's and get Gwen!

With all that settled in her mind, she paid the bill assuring the waitress that the food was perfectly fine, it was just her friend had been taken ill suddenly. The waitress helped them to the door and Pearl seemed to perk up a bit in the fresh air.

"Sorry, Ruby; I've spoilt your lunch. I just feel awful though, I'm exhausted!" Pearl felt dreadful for making Ruby miss lunch, but she couldn't have sat in there any longer, her stomach was still rolling, and her mouth felt dry and she could still taste the bile.

"It's fine, sweetheart, don't worry. I could do with missing a lunch or two anyway." Ruby laughed off her friend's apology. She got Pearl home and made her a cup of weak tea then, once she was lying on the tiny sofa in the living room, she nipped over to see if Edward was around. She saw one of the other porters and asked him if Edward was there, he pointed him out on the opposite platform. "Oy, Eddie!" he hollered, making Ruby jump in surprise, not just at his booming voice but the fact that he'd shouted 'Eddie'. Ruby had only ever known Edward to be called – well – Edward!

Edward looked over and seeing Ruby hurried over the stairway and down to the platform where she was waiting. "All right, Ruby?" he asked with a smile. "I thought you and Pearl were having lu…"

"She's not well, Edward," Ruby cut him off. "She's been sick everywhere and is feeling poorly, can you come home now? I don't want to leave her on her own, but I must get back to work and I'm going to pop by Norwich Union and let them know she won't be back this afternoon and possibly tomorrow as well," Ruby finished breathlessly. "Can you get someone to cover for you?"

"Yes, of course," said Edward, the smile replaced by a look of concern for his wife. "I'll have a word with Bill the Station Master, and I'll get my coat and lunch box and see you out the front in five minutes."

Ruby waited by the entrance until she saw Edward coming out of the side door. "Is it all right if I shoot off? I'll only be five minutes' late and I can make the time up tomorrow."

"Yes, of course, Ruby. You get along and I'll see to Pearl and thanks, Ruby, you're a diamond!" Edward said.

"Ha, ha, no I'm not, I'm a 'ruby'." laughed Ruby as she disappeared around the corner back to work.

Edward opened the back door quietly and was devastated to see Pearl lying there so ashen faced. Ruby had thoughtfully put the bucket from under the sink next to Pearl and the sour smell of vomit hit his nostrils. "Oh, my darling." He dropped to his knees beside Pearl and took her hand gently. "What can I get you, do you want some water, or maybe a cold flannel?"

Pearl looked at him weakly and said, "I'm so sorry, Edward, I feel awful, would you run up the hill and get Mum for me, please?"

Edward went off and soon arrived back with Gwen, bits of pastry still stuck to her fingers where she had been making a pie for tonight's tea. She took off her coat and asked Edward to put the kettle on while she sat by Pearl.

"Oh, Mum," Pearl said, desperately glad to see her mother. "I don't know what it is, but I keep being sick and the thought of food is making it worse. I don't think I can cook tea tonight for Edward, is there any chance he could eat with you and Dad?"

"Yes, of course," said Gwen. "Don't worry about that, he won't starve! How long have you been feeling like this, darling?" As she looked at Pearl an inkling of what could be wrong was beginning to form.

"Well, I didn't feel too clever when I got up to be honest, but I couldn't face breakfast and now I've made Ruby miss lunch. It took me an age to decide what to order as everything on the menu made me queasy, but I thought I'd be all right with Cod and Ch..." She leant over the bucket and was sick again. "Oh God," she groaned, "Will I have to see the doctor?"

"I think you will at some point, darling, yes." Gwen was reasonably sure now what the problem was. "When was the last time you had your 'monthlies'?" This last word was whispered in case Edward could hear.

"Hmm... Well, I missed last month for definite, but that was because of all the upset with Ruby and Jim having that awful row and him just going off for four days!" Pearl was still angry about that and was debating whether to tackle Jim or if it was best left alone for Ruby to sort out. "I can't remember the month before that but I'm sure I didn't miss it – or did I? Why are you asking

about them though, Mum… Oh! You don't think…"
The penny dropped and Pearl gawped at her mother who
now had a wide grin on her face, nodding.

"I'll get you an appointment with Dr Wilson
tomorrow, darling but I'm almost certain you're
pregnant!" Gwen called Edward in who was amazed to
see his mother-in-law and his wife both grinning like
Cheshire cats when half an hour ago he was convinced
Pearl was going to have to be rushed into hospital.

Gwen discreetly got up and went to make the tea
while Pearl told Edward what they suspected; the huge
cheer coming from the living room was enough for
Gwen to know Edward was over the moon! She had
been worried about Pearl as they had been married for a
while now and nothing seemed to be happening, but
now everything was going to be wonderful. She
couldn't wait to get home and tell John they were going
to be grandparents!

The doctor initially confirmed their suspicions and
asked Pearl to supply a sample to be tested at the
hospital; after an anxious week waiting the results were
confirmed – Pearl and Edward were having a baby!

Pearl was constantly ill with morning sickness –
which seemed to last most of the day – until one day
when she was around six months' pregnant it suddenly
stopped. From then on, she blossomed and her 'bump'
became enormous. Her mother was convinced it was
twins as her own mother was a twin and these things

skipped a generation, she importantly told everyone who listened.

All the neighbours were knitting away in whites and pastel colours to suit a boy or a girl and there were several offers of baby things to save them some money. Most of their Christmas presents that year were baby orientated; Eleanor had insisted on buying the pram and Gwen had to have a quiet word with her to ask her to hold off buying a single one – just in case.

Ruby was a constant visitor and, although she was secretly envious of Pearl – she'd always hoped they would go through their first pregnancy together – she was glad she and Jim had not become pregnant. Although to get pregnant, he would have to spend some time with her and actually be at home; he seemed to be off and about more times than he was at home now, she thought.

Pearl went into labour at thirty-two weeks and with Edward and John pacing up and down the corridor of the hospital, she finally gave birth to a little boy. Four minutes later the contractions had started again, and she was suddenly the mother of a little boy AND a little girl. Once the midwives had cleaned the tiny babies and wrapped them in shawls, they sorted Pearl out and Edward was allowed in. He gazed at Pearl with his two sleeping babies in her arms and thought he had never seen such a beautiful sight – he then promptly burst into tears!

Chapter 11
May 2018

Pearl was sitting in her usual chair on the patio, enjoying the warm weather and waiting for Susie to arrive. She heard the door open and looked up, delighted to see Susie was accompanied by Pete.

"Hello, my darlings, how lovely to see you both." She kissed them both and they settled in their chairs, thanking Michelle for bringing them a tray of tea and biscuits.

Pete looked at his mother and, although she still looked a bit peaky, he was reassured she was doing all right. "Susie has told me all the news, Mum. I played golf with Tony yesterday and he's told me about it too," he opened the conversation. "Apparently Ruby had asked Tony and Jack not to mention anything to us about her plans until she had spoken to you."

"Anyway, we have invited them all over for drinks on Friday to talk about what they are doing about going with Ruby to Switzerland etc.," Susie said, taking over from Pete. "Are you still determined to go with her?"

"Yes, love, I'd really like to be with her at the – you know, er – at the end." Pearl could feel the never-far-away tears welling up again. "I know she'll want the last few moments with her own family, but just to know I'm there will help, I think." She thought it was the least and the last thing she do for her oldest friend. "What do you think, darlings?"

"Well, there's a fair bit to organise, flights and accommodation and so on," said Susie practically. "But we can manage all of that for you. Obviously, you can't travel all that way on your own so one or both of us will come with you. We're probably best talking to the others first and seeing where they are staying and if there are rooms left there, if not somewhere close by so we can all be together."

"The one thing I want to know is when?" Pete said. "Exactly how long have we, or rather she, got left?"

"I seem to think it's three months, but I'm not totally sure. I don't think I took it all in to be honest, it was such a shock." Pearl suddenly burst into tears and her children jumped up from their seats to comfort her.

"It's all right, Mum, you have a good cry." Pete held her in his arms and let her sob.

She eventually stopped and Susie handed her some tissues. "It's been a terrible shock for us all," she said. "But we have to stand by Ruby's wishes and be there for her and support her family."

"I know, I feel so selfish as all I can think about it is what will I do without her?" Pearl was sniffling into her tissue but calming down now. "It's been so long since I've seen her and now, I'm going to lose her again – for good this time."

"Well, we'll know more on Friday so I'll either pop in to see you or I'll give you a ring. Is your mobile phone charged up?" Susie knew how much Pearl hated having the mobile, but it was a good thing to be able to reach her when she couldn't get there.

"Yes, Jill makes sure it's ready to go at any time," Pearl said.

They finished their tea and Susie distracted Pearl by showing her some photos she had taken of Harry at the park. "Ah, he's such a happy little chap, isn't he?" Pearl was enchanted by seeing him on the swings and braving the slide.

"Yes, he is a good boy. I hope he doesn't resent the new baby when it arrives, although he seems to take great delight in feeling Milly's tummy and asking if it's cooked yet!" Susie said. They all laughed, and Susie and Pete began to make their move to leave.

"So, I'll let you know when we find anything out, okay, Mum?" Susie bent to kiss her mother goodbye.

"Okay, dear, and thank you," said Pearl.

"Try not to worry too much, Mum," Pete said, kissing her soft cheek. "We'll get it sorted."

After they had gone, Pearl sat and collected her thoughts before heading back in. She wasn't up to anyone asking her any awkward questions; luckily the other residents were engrossed in a television programme and she was able to sit quietly near the back of the room. She wished Edward was here, he would know what to do. Oh, how she missed him at times like this, he was always her rock and so dependable. She knew they were lucky to have had such a good life together until he was cruelly taken.

After the lunch was finished Ted came over and said he had been talking to his grandchildren earlier and how marvellous it was to see their little faces.

Pearl looked at him and thought to herself, that's it – he has finally lost his marbles! His grandchildren lived in Australia for goodness sake! "Oh, Ted that's wonderful!" she said, not wanting to deflate him by telling him he couldn't possibly have seen them.

"Yes, it was lovely. Of course, they all talk like little Aussies now, but still, it was lovely – Bugger! I know what you're thinking, Pearl, you're thinking old Ted's finally lost it, aren't you?" he chuckled.

"No, no, Ted, I'm sure if you've seen them, then you have," Pearl said still not convinced.

"It's on this gadget my son brought in for me, you see. Hang on I'll fetch it and show you." Ted hurried off as fast as he could. Pearl sat and waited patiently amused now by whatever Ted was about to show her.

"Here it is, it's called a candle," he announced proudly.

"Erm, Ted? That is most definitely not a candle." Pearl looked at the rectangular shape he was holding. "Should I ask Jill to come over?" Pearl looked about to see if Jill was close by; she was a little worried now by Ted's strange behaviour.

"No, I'm fine," he said, wondering what Pearl was getting all het up about. "Here, look let me switch it on. It's got this thing on it called Swipe, or at least I think it's called that." Ted was now looking less confident as he fumbled about with the buttons, his stubby fingers not really suited for tiny switches and buttons. Pearl spotted Jill as she came into the lounge and with her eyes managed to attract her attention and Jill came over.

"Everything all right, Ted?" Jill asked.

"Yes, thanks, Jill." Ted looked up. "I'm just showing Pearl how to talk my grandchildren on my candle with the Swipe."

"Ah, right, Ted? It's called a *Kindle* and you spoke to your family on *Skype*." Jill was laughing as she offered to help Ted set it up.

"Well, bugger me, I knew it was summat like that." Ted looked affronted, then catching Pearl's eyes twinkling with laughter he started chuckling himself. "All this new-fangled stuff, it's a bugger, but it's marvellous, isn't it?"

They spent the next half an hour getting in touch with Ted's family again. He was absolutely delighted to be able to see his daughter and her three young children, and Pearl suspected they would be getting a lot of this Skype stuff over the next few weeks.

She resolved to tell Susie about it when she next came over or called. Who knows, maybe her grandchildren had one of these Kindle things and she would be able to see her family on it! She remembered how things were a lot different in her day, all the new technology was certainly a wonderful thing even if most of it was beyond her.

Chapter 12
April 1951

The first year after the twins were born was a tough time for Pearl and Edward. She thanked the Lord every day for her mother who was a constant support and gave advice in her gentle tones without upsetting anyone. Eleanor had come into her own and was besotted with her grandchildren; she showered them with gifts and offered to babysit several times so Edward and Pearl could have some time off for which they were grateful.

They were going to the local pub for a drink one evening, having taken Eleanor up on her offer. The bottles for the babies' feeds were made up ready and Gwen was going to pop down in an hour to make sure everything was okay. The twins were fast asleep – for once both at the same time. Pearl was a bit nervous about leaving her babies, but Edward persuaded her it would do them both good.

Pearl came down the stairs after checking on them one last time and Edward whistled softly, "Mrs Turner, you look absolutely stunning!"

Pearl laughed and said, "Well, this was the only dress I could fit into, I still have some baby weight to lose!" She was wearing a gold shift dress and gold coloured stilettos and had to admit she did feel pretty good!

Edward held her and kissed her, nuzzling into her neck.

"Let me just touch up my lipstick and I'm ready." She laughed, gently pushing him off – they would never get out at this rate!

Just as they were putting on their coats ready to leave, a frantic knock at the door sent Edward rushing to open it before the children woke up. "Ruby?" Edward peered out as Ruby came closer, looking a complete mess. "Whatever's happened? Pearl! It's Ruby, come in, come in my dear." Edward was concerned about her. Her eyes were red rimmed, and she was obviously in shock. She clutched a piece of paper in her hand.

Pearl took one look at Ruby and ushered her straight through into the kitchen. Edward wasn't sure if they were going out now, but it looked unlikely, he thought gloomily. He had been looking forward to a quiet pint – ah well, he took his coat off and sat chatting to his mother, one ear listening for any news coming from the kitchen.

"Oh, Pearl, he's gone, the rotten swine. I've told him to get his ratty case packed and I've chucked him out!" Ruby was angry and crying.

"Why, dear, what's he done?" Pearl knew exactly who Ruby was talking about, Jim! A sudden thought came to Pearl, "He hasn't hit you has he?" She held

Ruby's hand and hoped Edward couldn't hear; he would be straight round to punch Jim if he had touched Ruby!

"No, no, nothing like that, I found this." She handed Pearl the crumpled-up piece of paper she had been clutching. "How could he be like that? The cheating rotten pig! I hate him!" Ruby was crying again. Pearl read through the note and hugged her friend.

"Oh, my goodness, what a rat. To be honest, Ruby, I never really liked him; he always seemed a bit shifty!"

The note was from a woman called Barbara telling Jim how much she loved and missed him and to hurry home as she thought baby number three was going to make an appearance any day!

"I suppose he did it because he could get away it, my dear," Pearl said. "Look, I'd better tell Edward what's going on. We were just about to go for a drink, but I'll put the kettle on, and we'll have a cup of tea."

"Oh, Pearl, I'm so sorry, I know how much you were looking forward to having a night out." Ruby was immediately stricken with guilt, finally noticing Pearl was all dressed up.

"No, it's fine, don't worry. Look, I'll tell Edward and he can still go for a drink. Eleanor is here too, she was babysitting for us, so give me a minute and I'll be back." Pearl closed the kitchen door softly and went into the living room; she explained everything to Edward and Eleanor and encouraged Edward to still go out.

"Are you sure, darling? It seems so selfish to leave you on your own with Ruby like this." Edward wasn't sure he wanted to leave Pearl alone, but he *had* been looking forward to his drink!

"Yes, honestly, it's fine – and, Eleanor, thank you so much for coming down to babysit, do you think we could maybe do it another time?" Pearl hoped her mother-in-law wasn't going to be upset; she knew that as soon as they had left Eleanor would have crept upstairs and stood cooing over the babies' cots.

Eleanor had put her coat and was adjusting her scarf. "It's perfectly fine, dear, you see to Ruby and Edward can walk me home. Let me know when you want to arrange another time and I'll gladly babysit for you. Now, Edward, if we're quick you can get me home and then pop into Pearl's parents and see if John could manage a pint?" She winked at Edward who thought it was an excellent idea. Pearl hugged her gratefully, she really was a lovely lady and Pearl couldn't have asked for a better mother-in-law.

"Do you still want your mum to pop down, Pearl?" he called out as they made their way to the door.

"No, tell her not to worry and I'll catch up with her tomorrow." Pearl thought Ruby wouldn't want anyone to see her like this even though she was close to Gwen.

Edward saw his mother safely home and was more than pleased John was coming with him for a pint, who jumped up to get his coat. He had explained the situation to Gwen and John and Gwen had said to tell Pearl she was cooking a beef joint for dinner the next day and they were more than welcome to join them about two o'clock.

Pearl and Ruby sat and talked most of the evening in between feeding and looking after the twins. Ruby had brightened up a bit by the time Edward came home and they all sat and had a last cup of tea before Edward made sure Ruby was home safe and sound.

Jim had indeed packed his case and left, for which Edward was sincerely grateful. He wasn't sure he would have been able to keep his fists to himself if Jim had still been skulking around.

Over the following weeks it emerged that Jim had been arrested for bigamy and was to face the courts. Ruby was totally in the clear and, once she had been interviewed by the police, no further action was taken against her – she was the victim in all of this – although, as Pearl had pointed out, so was this Barbara and those poor little kiddies. Ruby was so ashamed she couldn't face going to work and the doctor had told her to take a week off until she was feeling better.

Ruby and Jim had rented the top floor of her aunt and uncle's house; her Aunt Maureen had said she was welcome to stay on and Uncle Tom had reduced her rent so she could manage it on her own. She was grateful she had somewhere to live, even though there were constant reminders of Jim around. She gradually got rid of all trace of him and her uncle helped her re-decorate to make it feel more like hers; it was amazing the difference a lick of paint and just moving the furniture about made.

The marriage was annulled, Ruby went back to work eventually, and she swore to Pearl she was off men completely from now on!

Within a year she was seeing Derek Clancy and her life began again!

Chapter 13
May 2018

Susie was busy putting out some nibbles and canapés for the drinks evening and Dan was opening bottles of red wine to let them breathe when Pete arrived.

"Hi, you two," he said, bending down to kiss his sister and shake hands with Dan. "Right, is there anything I can do to help?" he said, rubbing his hands together. He was slightly nervous how this evening would go, but he wanted to know all what was going on with Ruby.

"I think we are pretty much sorted thanks," Susie said, now laying out some napkins. "Ooh, could you put some ice in the bucket for the white wine, please?"

"Will do," Pete replied glad of something to do. He sorted out the ice bucket and Dan handed him a beer as they waited for the others to arrive. The doorbell went just on seven p.m. and Dan leapt up to answer it.

"Hi, Dan, hi, Susie, hi, Pete, good to see you." Tony and Jeannie came through into the kitchen, kissing Susie and shaking hands with Pete. Tony was tall, and at sixty-five with dark wavy hair flecked greyer now, he looked just like his father at around the same age. Jeannie, his wife, was also dark, but petite with amazing green eyes – it's the Irish in me, she would always say when anyone commented on them.

Jack and Maria followed, and the same pleasantries were exchanged. Jack was the epitome of tall, dark and handsome, he too had the same wavy hair – and the grey as Tony had – but he had a softer look about him that always reminded Susie of Ruby. Maria was a tall, cool blonde – a complete contrast to Jack – she used to be a model in her younger days and always had an air of sophistication surrounding her. She seemed aloof until you got to know her, but she was actually the life and soul of the party and she adored Jack.

"As it's so nice this evening, we thought we could sit on the patio," Susie said, picking up plates to carry though the French doors outside.

"Lovely idea," said Jeannie. "What do you want me to take, Susie? Sure, this all looks lovely!"

"Oh, thank you, hmm, just the bowl over on the side please, Jeannie, I think that's everything." Susie grabbed some more napkins and they made their way into the garden.

Dan had sorted out the drinks and they all sat and chinked wine glasses as Pete made a toast, "To long hot summers like we had when we were kids," he declared.

That opened the conversation and they spent the next hour swapping anecdotes of their childhoods and beach holidays; Jeannie and Maria roared with laughter at some of the tales Tony and Pete were relating. They then moved on to their own families' outings which they had sometimes shared as well. Susie and Dan had invited Tony and Jeannie along to their caravan with their children and Pete. Jack and Maria had popped up with their children and stayed a night or two with them as well, the children all squashed up in the same beds but happy after days in the sun and the sand.

"Ah, happy times, happy memories!" Pete said coming over a bit melancholy. There was a bit of an awkward silence as the conversation petered out and everyone sat around expectantly waiting for the real reason for the evening to be brought up.

"Okay," said Tony grasping the bull by the horns, "I guess we need to talk about Mum and her decision?" He looked around the table and cleared his throat. "First off, let me apologise for not saying anything before, and, Susie, I'm so sorry I didn't say anything during all the phone calls for your mum's party, Mum had asked me not to say anything to you guys as she wanted to tell Pearl herself, but I felt dreadful not telling you."

"We did ask her not to do it at the party, but she was adamant," Jeannie interjected.

"It's fine," Susie and Pete said in unison, then laughed.

Dan replenished everyone's drinks and Tony continued, "Yes, well, I still wanted to say something before, but you know Mum!"

"She wanted to get it all organised and sorted," Jack put in. "I also think she wanted Pearl to see how bad she had become and hoped Pearl wouldn't try and persuade her away from the idea, but to see that it was really the right thing to do – for Mum anyway," he tailed off lamely looking at his older brother to carry on.

"Right, yes, that's it exactly," said Tony. "To be honest, she had most of it worked out before she even mentioned it to any of us and Christ it was a shock, you know!" His voice started to thicken, and he cleared his throat again.

"So, where did she get the idea from in the first place?" Pete wanted to know.

Maria who had been sitting quietly sipping her wine and listening to the others fidgeted in her seat. "Ermm, I'm afraid it's all my fault," she said her lovely blue eyes clouding over.

"No, darling, it's not your fault at all, we all know what Mum's like." Jack took his wife's hand reassuringly.

"It's no one's fault," Susie said kindly. "We're not here to blame anyone or anything, we're just trying to understand and to see what we need to do next."

Maria smiled at the others and said, "I visited Ruby and she was telling me about how bad her arthritis had become. She was obviously in a lot of discomfort and the pills she was taking didn't seem to be helping that day." She took a deep breath. "So, I suggested she see a holistic healer. I thought they might be able to alleviate some of the pain with alternative medicine, you know. Well, I managed to get her an appointment for the following day providing we didn't mind waiting. They had the usual magazines and things to read and there were also some leaflets in the waiting room and Ruby must have picked one up while I nipped to the loo as I didn't see her pick one up. Anyway, she went in to see one of the practitioners and they seemed to think they could help her considerably. They offered her some capsaicin, curcumin and some cat's claw to start with and to see…"

"Do what!" Pete interrupted, thoroughly confused and thinking maybe he was drinking too much. Dan was pleased he asked as he too was stumped by what Maria was saying.

Oh, they're just some herbal supplements the practitioner prescribed for Ruby, "Maria explained.

"I've heard of one or two of them," Susie said. "They are supposed to have good results, has Ruby noticed any difference?"

"Yes, she has only been taking them a few months, but she says her knees are a little bit more supple," Maria said.

"So, why can't she just keep taking them or increasing the dose or whatever it is?" Pete asked. "Surely if they're making a difference then that's a good thing?"

"The thing is," Tony said picking up from Maria, "At Mum's age the improvement is only ever going to be minimal and with all the other problems she has it's not likely she'll recover enough to be fully functional."

"Mum said she had been diagnosed with early onset dementia," Susie said gently. It was all so sensitive, and she could feel her head starting to ache with it all, however, must Tony and Jack have come to terms with it – if indeed they had, certainly Tony seemed to be cut up about it still.

"Yes," Tony looked at Susie, "I think in the end that was probably the deciding factor; she was terrified of eventually not knowing us when we went to see her. I believe there is one old boy at the home she's in who is now in the second or third stage or whatever it is, and he has trouble remembering who the carers are and often refers to them as old relatives of his who have died years ago."

"Does that affect the doctor's decision, then?" Dan questioned, "You know, being of sound mind, etc?"

"At the moment she is still very much compos mentis, so she has been approved by the board of specialists to make the decision," Tony said. "Obviously, the brain cells will degenerate quite quickly and so it was decided to get everything in order sooner rather than later."

"When?" Susie almost squeaked, "I mean has a date been set yet?" Pete put his glass down and leaned forward, for some reason this was an important detail to him.

Tony cleared his throat a third time and Jeannie slipped her hand into his. "She is booked in for the first of September, erm, ... this year," he added unnecessarily. There was complete silence around the table at this point as they all digested what he had said.

"So soon," Pete murmured.

"Yes, old boy, as Tony says, time is of the essence here and once Mum makes her mind up there's no stopping her," Jack said trying to inject a light note to the proceedings.

"So, we've got what? A little over three months?" Susie was trying to sort out the practicalities in her head, "Are you all going?"

"It's just me and Jeannie, Jack and Maria who are going with Mum," Tony said. "We haven't said anything to the kids other than that we are taking Mum to Switzerland for a holiday as it's somewhere she's always wanted to go – like a bucket list thing."

"So, we'd appreciate it if you didn't say anything to your lot too – if that's okay with you?" Jack said apologetically looking at Susie and Dan.

"Absolutely," said Dan. "Maybe the best thing is just to say she passed away while on holiday – that sort of thing?"

"I suppose the fewer people who know the better it is," Pete said, nodding his head in agreement.

"Yes, it's not like we are hiding anything, we just think it's better all round for everyone not to worry and get upset," Tony said. "It's difficult enough dealing with it ourselves, let alone worrying about how everyone is feeling."

"Hmm," Susie was thinking out loud. "Milly's baby should be here by then, so Caroline will be pretty occupied by that and looking after Harry for her and Scott. She's the only one who might suspect something is going on, but hopefully she'll be kept busy." She continued, "And if we say Mum's going with Ruby to fulfil her bucket list, the others should be okay with that. I guess as it is short notice no one else will want to organise travel plans so soon, so that could be a blessing too."

"So, who is going to go with Pearl?" Pete had told Tony that Pearl wanted to go and support her friend. Jack looked over to Pete who had just opened some more wine, "You, Pete? Susie and Dan?"

"Yes, I think that should be enough, if you don't mind us tagging along?" Pete felt slightly awkward, as if they were intruding on someone else's grief even though no one had actually died – yet!

"Not at all, mate, don't feel awkward, in fact it will be nice to be all together one last time." Jack's face crumpled and he leapt up out of his seat and shot to the bathroom.

"Even though he says he's come to terms with it, I don't think he's dealing with it too well," Maria said. She stood up to go and check on Jack, but Jack came back just then and said sheepishly, "Sorry, folks, sometimes it just gets to you, you know? One minute I'm fine and I think, yep, I can do this and be strong for

Mum's sake, then I start blubbing like a bloody little boy missing his mum."

Tony clapped his hand on Jack's shoulder and said, "It's okay, bruv, we're all feeling the same so don't think any of us are finding this easy, but we will get through it."

"I'll start looking at flights and hotels in the morning," Dan said once the awkwardness had passed. They had all moved into the living room as it was getting a bit chilly outside now. He stole a glance at his watch and was shocked to see it was eleven thirty., "So, how does it work? Are you staying in the, er – clinic with Ruby or are you booked in a hotel locally? If you can let me have the address and your flight details, I can sync them to ours."

"I'll email everything over to you when we get home, then you can get organised. We are staying in a little guest house about a mile away from the clinic, there might be room there but if not, there are several other little places you could try." He too looked at his watch, "Right, we'd better push off and let you guys get to bed, it's a lot to take in, isn't it?"

"Thank you so much for coming and letting us know," Susie said, retrieving jackets and handing them to the others who had stood ready to leave.

"Thank you for having us." Jeannie kissed Susie and hugged her, they all said their goodbyes and Susie and Dan cleared up in near silence.

Dan finally spoke, "You all right, darling? Strange evening, wasn't it?"

"Totally bizarre and surreal, I can't imagine how they're feeling about it all, well, except Jack of course, he's always worn his heart on his sleeve!" Susie said. She was completely exhausted by it all, "Come on, love, leave the rest, I'll do it in the morning, let's get to bed and try and get some sleep."

Chapter 14
May 2018

Caroline had indeed been thinking about her grandmother's party. As she and Tim had left with Milly and Harry, she was wondering why Tony and the others hadn't turned up. Oh, she knew all about Ruby arriving was the surprise, but she had assumed Tony, Jack and their wives at least would have been there or turned up a bit later. She waited until Tim had carried a sleepy Harry in and up the stairs and they had got Milly settled with a cup of tea before they left to drive home.

"Thanks, Mum, I'm fine now. I might even have a little nap myself now Harry's gone off," Milly said wearily, her ankles were a bit swollen and she was feeling tired. "It was a lovely day though, wasn't it? The look on Great-Grandma's face when Auntie Ruby came in was priceless!"

"Yes, she certainly enjoyed it. Even though she always tells everyone not to bother, she was so pleased we all made the effort," Caroline said bending to kiss her daughter as she lay on the sofa with her feet up. "We'll see ourselves out, darling, you stay there and rest.

"I think Harry charmed the pants off everybody!" Tim said laughing as he too bent to say goodbye to Milly.

"I'll call you tomorrow, darling," Caroline called out as they were closing the door behind them.

"Mmm... Okay, lovely ... bye." Milly was almost asleep by then.

As soon as Tim started the car up Caroline said, "Did you think it strange Uncle Tony and the others weren't there?"

"Well," Tim said thoughtfully, he knew what a worrier his wife could be. "I suppose as Ruby was the surprise guest that was all that was really important," he said diplomatically, although now she had mentioned it, he thought it was probably a bit odd. Tony and Jack were quite close to Pearl and even if one of them couldn't make it the other one would have been there; it was unusual for them both not to appear.

"Hmm... yes, I guess you're right, it just seems odd that's all." Caroline resolved to speak to Susie when she saw her for coffee later in the week; they usually tried to catch up once a week. They had a close relationship and Caroline knew her mum would tell her if anything was amiss.

They had met up on the day Susie had taken Harry to the park and Susie was unusually quiet. Caroline knew she had been to see her gran earlier in the day and was keen to find out what, if anything was going on. Susie seemed pre-occupied and wasn't giving anything away other than to say that Ruby had wanted to surprise Pearl on her own and Ruby's sons had decided not to go so she and Pearl could have some time alone; Caroline didn't buy it, but she could see that trying to press her mother any further wasn't helping. Susie remained tight lipped.

Caroline had spoken to her siblings, but Fleur hadn't noticed anything different and Josh wasn't even there, so she was unable to find out more. She decided to let it go for now.

Two weeks later she had far more important things to worry about as Milly had gone into premature labour and she was rushing back and forth to the hospital and looking after Harry; Milly's baby daughter arrived in the early hours weighing just under five pounds and was whisked away to the special care unit for a few days. They hadn't decided on a name yet, but Caroline was hoping for something old fashioned – like Amelia maybe!

Milly was discharged from hospital after a week, the baby's weight had gone up and the doctors were satisfied with her progress.

Caroline and Tim were waiting at their house with Harry who was clutching a tiny teddy to give to his new sister. Scott pulled up onto the drive and Tim went to the kitchen to open the champagne.

"Everyone, please meet Olivia!" Milly announced proudly as Scott came in with the tiny scrap bundled in her car seat. Caroline thought Olivia was much nicer than Amelia and approved wholeheartedly.

The champagne was opened, and glasses passed round; Milly only had a tiny sip as she was breast feeding. Caroline took a video on her phone of Harry passing the teddy to his new sister, albeit reluctantly as he seemed to have taken a liking to it himself, he tried to keep it and offer her one of his old toy cars instead, but she didn't seem interested in anything. Harry soon left the others to it and played in the other part of the room with his favourite cars – keeping one eye on the new baby.

Susie and Dan instantly fell in love with the tiny baby when Milly, Scott and Harry came to visit. Caroline and Tim had popped in as well, so there was quite a houseful. Susie made sure to take lots of pictures to show her mother when she visited later in the week; Pearl had had a summer cold and had told Susie it might be best if Milly didn't come over for a week or two.

Caroline had sent Susie the video of Harry and Olivia and Susie knew Pearl would be thrilled to see it. Milly asked her to check when it would be okay to go and said they would visit Pearl when her cold was better. She knew her great grandma would love to see Olivia and all the other old ducks at the home would be delighted.

The arrival of Olivia had come at just the right time, Dan thought, gazing adoringly at his great-granddaughter. Tony had emailed him all the information the morning following the drinks party and over the following days he had booked the flights for himself, Susie, Pete and Pearl. He had managed to get an assisted ticket for Pearl so they would be able to board first, and a wheelchair would be made available if she needed it. Pearl was still quite sprightly, but she did tire easily so it was reassuring to know help was there. Tony had suggested getting it if he could as, obviously, they had booked one for Ruby.

They would be arriving the day after Tony, Jack and the others which again Dan thought was better as it would give them time to settle in. They had all planned to meet up on the evening of the thirtieth of August – two days before Ruby went to the clinic. They would be leaving on the third of September, although Tony and Jack would stay on until the fourth to sort out the formalities or whatever else was required.

The guesthouse the others were staying in was full so he had booked another which was only five minutes' walk away from them; he thought afterwards that it was a good thing as it meant they could all have some space if they needed it, but they were close enough to meet up for drinks or whatever.

Pete had paid for his and Pearl's tickets, waving off Susie's protests, saying she needed every penny now to spend on her great-granddaughter!

Dan would normally have been looking forward to arranging for a little jaunt away. He and Susie quite often just booked something last minute and off they went, but this time was completely different.

"So," said Dan softly to a sleeping Olivia, "Everything is ready for the big day, but how the hell can I say goodbye to someone I've known and loved for over forty years and support my darling wife at the same time as my heart is breaking, hmm...?" He looked at Olivia and a new life beginning and thought of Ruby as her life was about to end. She wriggled in his lap and suddenly opened her eyes – it startled him a bit as she looked like she knew what he was talking about!

Susie came over and asked him if he was okay. "Yes, I'm fine, darling, although I think this little one is getting ready for some lunch!" Dan passed the baby back to Milly and, as she was breast feeding, he thought it best to disappear for a bit. He decided to take Harry out for an ice cream and a trip to the park, Scott joined them, and they spent a happy hour or so eating their ices and feeding the ducks. They chatted about nothing in particular and as Scott didn't know anything, he didn't ask any questions, and Dan was able to enjoy it without the constant burden he felt.

Scott and Milly had had been together for five years and Dan couldn't have wished for a nicer chap to be with his granddaughter. They seemed very happy together and they all doted on Harry without spoiling him too much. He looked at Scott pushing Harry on the swings; Harry certainly took after his dad, Dan thought. Scott was tall with sandy hair cut short and the hours he spent in the gym were evident in his trim waist and toned arms. He wore a tee shirt and jeans and Dan sucked in his stomach and thought maybe he should go to the gym or give up the wine!

Susie seemed to maintain her petite figure though and she could drink almost as much as him! Ah, well, he thought, at nearly seventy he wasn't in bad shape. With that Harry jumped off the swing and raced over to Dan who picked him up and swung him round, "Are you ready to go back, young man?" Dan asked him,

"Yes," Harry nodded. "See baby?" he said solemnly. Dan chuckled and replied that, yes, they were indeed going to see the baby – they would all be all right, he thought, as they walked back to the house.

Chapter 15
June 2018

Susie arrived at Willow Lodge just before eleven o'clock as usual. She stopped and had a word with Jill before making her way to her mother's room. Pearl had decided to stay inside today, and Susie was relieved to see her dressed and sitting in her armchair with the radio on playing softly.

"Hello, my darling," Pearl said, happy to see Susie, "I hope you've got lots of photos of the baby to show me? I have a bag in the corner of matinee jackets and mittens Betty has knitted so don't forget to take them when you leave."

"Oh, how lovely!" Susie exclaimed as she had a look at the top two or three beautifully knitted things. "She's so clever! I'll pop in and thank her before I go, how are you feeling, Mum?" she asked. She could see her mother was definitely on the mend; the last time she had called Pearl was looking very pale and her eyes were very heavy, but today she looked much brighter and had her lipstick on as usual!

"I'm much better now, thank you, darling. It was a nasty cold, but it seems to be on the way out. thank goodness. I still have a chesty cough, but the doctor is coming tomorrow so, hopefully, he'll give me the all clear and I can have visitors again." Pearl smiled at Susie and was glad she was feeling better. "So, where are these pictures then? And what other news is there?"

Susie opened her phone and showed Pearl all the photos she had taken of Olivia.

"Oh, my, look at her, she is so tiny!" Pearl said, "Look at her tiny fingers! What was her weight again?"

"She was just under five pounds when she was born, but she's now put on a couple of ounces so she's doing really well," Susie said proudly. "Here, have a look at this video of Harry giving her a present; Caroline took it and sent it to me so I could show you." She fiddled with the volume and started the video; Pearl was enchanted to see it and it reminded her of Ted and his 'candle'!

"Oh, Susie, I have to tell you about Ted and the other week, he made me laugh so much!" Pearl said, starting to giggle at the memory.

"He didn't propose to you, did he?" Susie said in mock horror.

"Ha, ha, no, not that, well, not yet anyway." Pearl winked at her daughter. "Don't worry, I have no intention of marrying Ted or anybody anytime soon," she said determinedly.

"Well, you know if you ever did decide to marry again Pete and I would support you, Mum, you know that, don't you?" Susie said gently. It wasn't something that had come up before but if her mum was lonely and

115

needed some companionship then she was perfectly happy for her to find it.

"Ah, thank you, darling, but rest assured I am very happy on my own. I could never replace your dad, so I'm not even going to try." Pearl's eyes misted over as they always did when she thought of Edward. "Now," she said before she started blubbing, "Let me tell you about Ted!"

They were both laughing so much by the time Pearl had finished telling her about the 'candle' and then how to 'swipe' that Susie was concerned for her mother as she went into a coughing fit.

"I'm fine," Pearl said, waving her away. "It still tickles me every time I think of it, but old Ted is as proud as punch to be able to speak to his daughter and grandkids in Australia. It got me thinking, I was wondering does Simon have one of these Kindle things. Or anyone else got one? I'll tell you why, I was thinking if any of Ruby's family had one there might be a way to hook them up or whatever it is you do, and I could have a chat with Ruby without her having to travel over here or me over there. What do you think, darling?"

"Oh, that's a brilliant idea! I'm pretty sure we've got one at home somewhere. I'll ask Dan tonight and, if we have, I'll speak to Tony and see if we can organise something. Leave it with me, Mum, and I'll sort it out for you. It'll be lovely for you and Ruby to have a chat," Susie said. "Now, I'd better fill you in on all the news from the other evening, hadn't I?"

They spent the next half hour discussing all the plans that had been made and Pearl was confident Susie and Dan had it all in hand. "So, Tony and Jack are all right with me going then?" she asked apprehensively.

"Yes, of course, they know how long you two have been friends and, as Jack pointed out, you are more like sisters really, so they are more than happy for you and us to go," Susie said reassuringly. "Now, I can hear the lunch things being put out, so I shall shoot off and I'll let you know if Dan has a 'candle'!" They both roared with laughter again as Susie stood to go. "I'll just pop into Betty, then I'll be off. Is there anything you need before I go?"

"No, dear, I'm fine, it was lovely to see you and please tell Milly I should be all right if she wants to pop over next week."

Susie left and Pearl freshened up before lunch. After lunch, Jill had a free hour and asked Pearl if she fancied a gentle walk in the grounds to get some fresh air. Pearl was warm in her cardigan as they strolled along the path and she regaled Jill with the news of Milly and Olivia. "Ah, lovely," said Jill. "I'm so pleased everything is okay, it must have been a worry for them with Milly going into labour so early," she said.

"Yes, it was. You know my twins were born at thirty-two weeks: Peter was four pounds four ounces and Susie was four pounds two ounces, so they were a good size really, but so tiny! Edward was afraid to hold them at first, he was sure he might break one!" Pearl chuckled at the memory. "He soon had to get the hang of it, though. With two hungry babies all the time I certainly couldn't manage on my own. Thank the stars my mother was able to help out as much as she did and Ruby, of course, she was a tremendous help to us in the early days."

"Have you heard from Ruby since your birthday party?" Jill asked cautiously. She still wasn't aware of all that had happened, and she didn't want to upset Pearl by asking awkward questions.

"No, I haven't spoken to her yet." Pearl went on to tell Jill about her idea to Skype Ruby if they could get two Kindles to hook up. "Well, if Susie doesn't have one but Ruby's family can get hold of one, I'm sure Ted would lend you his, after all it was, he that started all this," she laughed.

"Ooh, yes, I hadn't thought of that. Good idea, Jill, I'll see what Susie says and then we can ask Ted if not." They made their way back in and Jill organised the inevitable cup of tea for Pearl.

All this talk of babies, Pearl thought later, transported her back to when her babies were born and how quickly they soon grew. They were never blessed with any more children, but she was so, so grateful for the two she had.

Chapter 16
September 1954

"Right, you two, are you ready? Have you got everything?" Pearl was fighting to hold back the tears as she stood at the school gates, it was the twins' first day and she was more nervous than they were.

"I'm ready, Mummy," said Susie.

"And me, too," said Pete.

They both looked adorable in their school uniforms, Pete already half a head taller than Susie at four and a half. "Okay then well off you go – oh wait, here's your dad." Pearl stopped them as she saw Edward racing up the road.

"Phew!" Edward said breathlessly, "I just made it!"

"I didn't think you were coming." Pearl was relieved to see him.

"Ah, I wouldn't miss this for the world," Edward said beaming at his children. "My, you both look so smart, are you ready?"

"Yes," they replied in unison, then stopped again as Ruby came rushing up.

"Sorry, sorry, I'm late, I couldn't get Anthony to settle and Derek had to take over so I could get away."

"We are a bit early, so don't worry, but if they don't get a move on soon then they will be late." Pearl was pleased Ruby had made it; she knew she would have wanted to be here. Since Ruby and Derek had married and now had Anthony who was just over a year old, they hadn't seen each other too often but their strong bond was still in place and, whenever they could, they would meet up – usually at one another's houses for a cuppa and a catch up.

"Mummy? We need to go in now." Susie was hopping up and down.

"Yes, dear, of course. Right, come on, let's go. Wave bye, bye to Daddy and Auntie Ruby." Pearl took their hands and led them into school.

Ruby and Edward were chatting by the gates when Pearl returned; she put her tissue in her pocket and smiled brightly at them both.

"Come on, darling, they will be fine." Edward put his arm around Pearl as they walked away.

"Yes, I know, I'm just soft!" Pearl said, her voice choked with emotion.

"Ah, you've always been the softie, sweetheart," Ruby, said giving Pearl a hug. "Right, I've got to love you and leave you and get back to save Derek from Anthony's screaming – I think he's getting some back teeth through! I'll pop round tomorrow while the twins are at school if you like, Pearl?"

"Oh, yes that will be perfect; I have some Victoria sponge left over that needs eating up." Pearl had cheered up now.

"Excellent! Okay, bye, see you tomorrow." And Ruby was off.

"What time do you have to be back?" Pearl said to Edward as they made their way home. They had moved from the little cottage two years ago and now lived in a nice semi-detached house on Carrow Road. They were still close enough for Edward to get to work but it was nice to have a bigger garden now the children were growing up.

"I'm all right for another quarter of an hour or so," said Edward. "I've nipped out in between trains and Mick is covering for me if I'm a bit late back. I won't go back until I know you're all right though." Edward was still a porter for the railway, the pay wasn't brilliant, but it was a steady job and he enjoyed it.

"I'm fine really, love, it was just seeing their little faces all shiny and excited. I think Susie is a bit fearful, but Pete didn't look worried by it all." Pearl was back to normal now and rather pleased with herself for not crumbling completely as she thought she might do.

"Ha, ha yes, for twins they are like chalk and cheese." Edward laughed, "Right then, love, if you're sure you're okay, I'll get back and relieve Mick. Why don't you go to your mum's and have a cup of tea?"

"I might do. I've got the washing to do though and it's looking like it might be dry all day, so I'll get that on the line first, then see after that." Pearl had left a few jobs to keep her busy while she was on her own. She was going to start working part time back at her old place in the new year and she was both excited and nervous at the same time.

They kissed each other and Pearl walked home. She nearly lost her resolve when the house was so silent and empty, but she switched on the radio and got on with the washing. Before she knew it, it was time to collect the children from school and start preparing tea for her family.

The following day Ruby came around for a cup of tea and they happily whiled away the morning with Tony playing with some of the twins' old toys. They had a good catch up and Pearl could see how happy Ruby was with Derek, and now she had a baby of her own she was glowing. Pearl shuddered when she thought of Ruby's first 'husband' Jim. Derek was aware of what had happened with him, but no one spoke his name at all.

"I love this house, Pearl," Ruby said admiringly. "You have made it look really lovely,"

"Thank you. Sweetheart. I'm lucky that Edward is a dab hand with a hammer and nails; he's put up loads of shelving units for the twins' bedrooms and he's starting on the kitchen cupboards after Christmas. I told him to leave it until then as it will make such a mess and I can't cook the turkey with half the kitchen missing!"

Pearl was looking forward to Christmas more than ever this year. In previous years they had gone to Gwen and John's, but now the house was getting straight they had invited her parents and Eleanor to Christmas lunch. Edward suspected Eleanor might turn up with her new beau; she had been hinting as such and Pearl had said the more the merrier. The new dining room table was being delivered at the end of October and would seat them all comfortably.

"Are you going to Derek's parents this year, dear?" Pearl asked Ruby.

"Yes, we had last year with mine so it's only fair we go to Derek's lot this year. I'm not sure Derek's mum likes me, to be honest, being married before and all, but she's pleasant enough so it'll be all right," Ruby said with a grimace.

"Ah, if anyone can win her over, it's you, sweetheart!" Pearl got up to make some more tea and gave her friend a warm hug.

"You know, I'm so glad Miss Masters put us together all those years ago, we've been through some stuff together, haven't we?" Ruby said hugging her back, "Friends to the end – remember?"

"We certainly have, and we still have the rest of our lives to look forward to!" Pearl said cheerily. "And definitely friends to the end."

After another cup of tea Anthony was getting a bit fractious. "I'm going to get off now, Pearl, and put this one down for his nap," Ruby said, picking up the wriggling little boy.

"He's been as good as gold all morning, bless him," Pearl said fondly as she kissed his soft little cheek. "You're going to be a heartbreaker when you grow up, young man." She ruffled his hair and Ruby put his coat on, said goodbye and they made their way home.

Later that afternoon Pearl was peeling the potatoes for tea, the twins were playing in the garden where she could see them, and she thought how grateful she was for her life. She couldn't ever imagine life without her children, her beloved Edward and her best friend Ruby, whatever would she do without them?

Chapter 17
June 2018

Tony sat back with a glass of whisky and looked at Jack in the armchair opposite.

"I'm glad we spoke to Susie, Dan and Pete last week, aren't you?" Jack said, taking a sip of his own glass and nodding appreciatively. "Glenfiddich twelve-year-old single malt? Am I right?"

"Ha, ha, no fooling you, little brother! You know your whiskies as well as I do! Yes, you're right," Tony said, savouring his drink and putting the bottle on the table from behind his chair where he had hidden it from Jack. "Yes, it was good to talk to them. I was feeling awful keeping it from Susie during all those calls, but it was what Mum wanted." He continued, "Pointless, I know, but I was kind of hoping that old Pearl would have been able to talk Mum out of it!"

"Yep, me too, but I don't think any of us could have changed her mind. You know what she's like once her mind is made up, she's always been the same!" Jack said thoughtfully. "Christ, it's still taking some getting used to though, isn't it? I keep thinking what the hell is it going to be like, you know, watching her... you know?" He broke off unable to carry on.

"I know, mate, I know, I keep thinking the same too, but we'll get through it. We have to for Mum's sake, and it could be worse, at least we get to say goodbye and not watch her suffer with cancer or something, or she could have been run over or in a car crash then we would never get the chance to say goodbye. Think how shitty that must be for the poor bastards who have to live with that! This way, apparently, it's supposed to be what they call 'a good death'," Tony said, doing quotation marks with his free fingers.

"I know, it could be worse, but it's still going to be hard, sitting there holding her hand while she slips aw…" He put his glass down and buried his face in his hands.

"Come on, mate, you'll be fine. It will be tough, but from what the quacks say it will be quite quick and she won't be in any more pain, she'll just drift off to sleep and that'll be it." Tony's voice shook at that point. He took another gulp of his drink and felt the warming sensation hit his belly.

"I think Pete feels as if he's intruding on our grief," Jack said. "I, for one, am actually glad they will be there. We've always done stuff together, so it makes sense that we're altogether now for the last bit – so to speak."

"And don't forget they have all known Mum longer than we have, as they are older than us!" Tony said, getting up and pouring another inch for Jack. "It's really going to tough on Pearl and at her age too; you know

Susie said that when her mum said she was going with Mum she nearly fainted!"

"Bloody hell! That would be just typical of them wouldn't it, to go together." Jack laughed then said thoughtfully, "You don't think that's the real reason Pearl is going, do you?"

"I don't see how she can, mate. Look at all that crap Mum had to go through to get the approvals, etc. Pearl won't be able to get that sorted in time, so no, I think she just wants to be there for Mum really." Tony had thought the same as Jack, but it wasn't practical, and he had dismissed the thought.

"So, they started out as friends in school, Mum said." Jack had heard the story of how the teacher had put them together as their names went together.

"Yeah, they were sat next to each other because their names were both precious gems!" Tony laughed.

"I'm glad they didn't carry on the trend and give us lot jewel names!" Jack said.

"I think they were just the popular names of the day," Tony said. "Thank god! Can you imagine me being Onyx or some shit!" Jack burst out laughing.

"Ha, ha, yeah, Susie and Pete would be Amethyst, and Beryl and we would have been Onyx and Agate!" They were both roaring with laughter when Jeannie came in, drying her hands on a tea towel, to see what was making them make so much noise.

"Dinner's ready, love," she said, smiling at the brothers and joining in with the laughter. "What's tickled you two, then? Are you staying for a bite to eat, Jack? There's plenty."

Jack had calmed down a bit now and replied, "Oh, thanks, Jeannie, but Maria should be here in a minute." He checked his watch for confirmation. "Yes, she should be on her way. Kirsty's friend's baby shower should be nearly done, then we are going to the cinema and we'll get something to eat after that."

"Ooh, that reminds me, I must tell Maria about Megan's baby shower – it's next week," she said. "Don't let me forget, Tony, will you?"

"You two go and eat, I'll finish my drink and wait for Maria if that's okay?" Jack didn't want to gulp it down otherwise he would be feeling too tipsy for the film, and he certainly wasn't leaving a twelve-year-old single malt!

"If you're sure?" Tony said, draining his glass and thinking that would do him for the night. He needed to eat something soon though, otherwise he would feel it in the morning.

"Yeah, its fine, she'll be here in the next five min…" Jack was cut off by the doorbell ringing. "And here she is, spot on time!"

After the usual greetings and goodbyes and the confirmation that Maria would be going to the baby shower, Tony and Jeannie sat down to eat.

"I didn't open any wine as I wasn't sure if you wanted any after the whisky," Jeannie said as they started on the dinner.

"No, love, to be honest I think orange juice is fine. I wasn't expecting Jack to pop in so I wouldn't have had the whisky normally, but he looked in need of a stiffener!" Tony said, pouring them both a glass of the juice.

"So, how is he?" Jeannie said in her soft Irish lilt, at sixty-three she had lived most of her adult life in the UK, but the accent was still there. "I heard you two laughing – what was that about?" Tony told her about the gem's theory, and she laughed as she said, "Hmm, I'm not sure I could ever marry anyone called Onyx!"

"Yes, it was good to see him laughing. You know, love, this whole thing has really got to him, as it has all of us, I know, but he seems to be all right one minute then the next he's falling apart," Tony said, concerned for his brother.

"He's in the grieving process, love," Jeannie said. "It will take him some time for sure. Remember when Mam was ill, and we were flying backwards and forwards to Dublin? How awful it was every time we got there, and she had gone downhill a bit more, then the final days and we couldn't do anything, just felt so bloody useless?" Jeannie's eyes clouded as she remembered her mother's demise four years ago. "Ah, sure, she was on the morphine, but it was hell watching it happen, at least you'll be spared all that."

Tony took Jeannie's hand and said, "Yes, I remember, and, to be honest, when you pointed it out to me when Mum told us of her plans, I think it was that

that made me come around. I tried explaining it to Jack, you know, she could go under a bus or in a car crash or something and he does agree this is the best way. It's just hard sitting about waiting and knowing what's going to happen as the clock ticks down!"

"It will be tough for you both. At least you'll have Susie and Pete for support and Dan, of course, he's a tower of strength." Jeannie got up to clear the plates. "Do you want any dessert? There's some ice cream, if you fancy it?"

"Err, no, not on top of the booze, thanks, love." Tony started to clear the table. "I'll give it a miss. Shall we watch that programme we recorded the other day and get that out of the way?"

"Yes, good idea, give me five minutes and I'll be in." Jeannie thought the distraction would do them both good and hopefully Tony would sleep a bit better tonight.

Jack and Maria chatted on the way to the Riverside where the multi-screen cinema was; Jack asked how the baby shower went and Maria said it was lovely. Kirsty's friend Lou was having a boy and she described the gender reveal cupcakes they had.

"Another thing we've adopted from the Americans," Jack said. "They certainly didn't have all this years ago, still I suppose it's good to be prepared. I wonder if this will make Kirsty and Jordan want to have one now?" He was looking forward to becoming a granddad though he wasn't sure if Maria was ready to be called Nana anytime soon!

"I think they are waiting until Jordan gets this promotion he's after, then they will be better off money wise," Maria replied. "There's plenty of time for us to be grandparents – don't worry!"

They watched the film, decided it was worth going to see after all and grabbed some fish and chips on the way home. Jack fell into a dream-filled sleep that night, full of babies going around administering drugs to all the old people they met. He woke in the morning feeling quite disturbed by it all; he told himself it was just a dream and nothing to worry about.

Chapter 18
June 2018

Susie was searching through the little room upstairs Dan used as a study. "Are you sure it's in one of these drawers?" she called to Dan, who was on his hands and knees looking in the wardrobe in their room.

"I thought that's where it was," came the muffled reply. "If not there, maybe it's stashed in one of the suitcases from when we went to Italy last month, I'll have to go up in the blasted loft and check!"

"Hang on," said Susie, "The little cabin bags are in here, it might be in the side pocket – Aha! Found it!" she said triumphantly.

"Perfect," Dan said, relieved he didn't have to go into the loft; his old knees didn't like the climb up there!

"It's a bit dusty and it will need charging, but I reckon it will be perfect!" Susie handed the Kindle to Dan and switched it on.

"Yep it's down to about fifteen per cent," he said. "It won't take anytime at all to get it up and running, obviously they have Wi-Fi at the home so that won't be a problem. I'll give Tony a ring later and see if he's had any luck getting hold of one. It's a marvellous idea for your mum and Ruby to be able to chat on Skype, it will probably do them both good."

"Definitely! And it will give Mum something to talk about other than old Arthur's back problems or Hilda's bowel movements!" Susie laughed.

"Eww!" said Dan, "Too much information, thank you!"

"Right, well now we've found the Kindle, do you want a coffee before we go shopping or should we be decadent and buy one when we're out?" Susie was washing her hands and wandered through to where Dan was still in the bedroom.

"Oh, let's go mad and buy one out – my treat!" Dan said. "I'm just going to change my shirt then I'm all yours."

Once the shopping was done and they were in Starbucks having their coffee, Dan looked up and saw Tony walking past. He tapped on the window and Tony's face lit up when he saw them. He ordered himself a latte and made his way to where they were sitting.

"I was going to ring you later," Dan said. "Susie found the Kindle; we hadn't used it since the last holiday, so it was still in the suitcase. It's on charge so it will be ready to go by tomorrow. Did you have any luck getting hold of one?"

"Yes, Maddie let us have her one. She said she hardly ever uses it so Mum can have it for as long as she wants – well, until you know, until she doesn't need it –

Jesus! It's so bloody awkward, isn't it?" he grinned sheepishly at Susie and Dan.

"It's fine, Tony, it's only us, so you don't have to feel awkward at all. You can say whatever you like, and it will still be fine." Susie gave him a reassuring smile.

"Yeah, I know, thanks, Susie." Tony sipped his latte. "So, what I plan to do is go over to see Mum tomorrow and show her what she has to do – that might take some time!" he laughed.

"Ah, okay, well we can go and see Mum tomorrow too if you like and we can maybe get them started? What time are you heading over there?" Susie asked.

"It'll probably be about three-ish, so if you get to Willow Lodge around the same time, I'll give you a ring when we are ready to try it out. How does that sound?" Tony asked. He was actually looking forward to being able to do something for his mum, only a small thing but it made him feel better.

"Excellent!" Dan said. "Well, that's all sorted, I can't wait to see their faces when they realise, they can see each other in real time.

"Oh, dear!" Susie said as the thought hit her. "Can you imagine Mum? I'd better warn her that Ruby will be able to see her clearly, she'll want to make sure she has her lipstick at the ready!" They all laughed at that and finished their coffees before heading their separate ways.

The following afternoon, Susie and Dan were sat with Pearl chatting when Dan's phone rang. "Hello, mate, are you all set? We've got it all set up here, so ready when you are." Dan looked at Pearl who was excited about seeing Ruby but not one hundred percent sure how it was all happening. Suddenly the Kindle rang and there on the screen she could see Tony!

"Yoo hoo, Pearl, I can see you! Can you see me?" Tony's voice came through and he was waving at Pearl.

"Oh, HELLO, DEAR, HOW ARE YOU?" Pearl shouted at him.

"You don't need to shout, Mum," Susie said. "It's got speakers so they can hear you clearly, just talk in your normal voice."

"Sorry, dear," Pearl said contrite. "This might take some getting use…" she broke off suddenly for there on the screen was Ruby's smiling face!

"Oh, my word, there she is. Look, Susie, its Ruby. Hello, my dear, how are you?" Pearl was overcome with excitement and her voice wavered with emotion.

"All the better for seeing you, darling Pearl." Ruby beamed at her, though her voice too was emotional. "What a brilliant idea this is, we can have little chats whenever we like now."

"It was Ted who gave me the idea," Pearl said and went on to explain to Ruby what Ted had shown her and talking to Australia.

"Right then, we'll leave you to it, Mum," Susie said. "When you're finished, just press the button on the top and it will disconnect you. If you get any problems, I'm sure Jill or Michelle will be able to help."

"Thank you so much for doing this." Pearl gave Susie and Dan a hug. "I can't begin to tell you how much this means."

"You are very welcome," Dan said and waved to Tony "Right, we're off, mate, thanks again and we'll catch up with you later."

"Yes, Mum's got the hang of it here, so I'm going to push off too, see you soon." Tony disappeared from the screen.

When it was just Pearl and Ruby left, they looked at one another and burst out laughing.

"Isn't this marvellous?" Ruby said. "Can you see me okay?"

"Yes, dear, I can see you, can you see me all right?" Pearl looked intently at the screen so Ruby could see her clearly.

"Ha, ha, yes, right now we can both see each other. How are you? Have you seen Milly and the new baby yet? I can't wait to hear all the news!" Ruby was the most animated she had been in weeks; it was so nice to catch up with Pearl. They hadn't really had long enough the other weekend and she felt bad for spoiling Pearl's party with her news.

"I'm well, dear, I have been getting over a particularly bothersome cold so I haven't seen the baby yet, but Susie has shown me some photos and now I'm feeling better they will pop down and see me next week. If we can get this going again you could see her for yourself, how would that be?" Pearl thought this was so much better than writing a letter. She knew the young people nowadays all sent texts – whatever they were – to one another but she would rather chat face to face.

"Ooh! Yes, that would be perfect, I'd love to see her, and maybe when Megan has had hers, we can do the same thing? Pearl? I'm so sorry I told you what I'm doing at your party, it was wrong of me and I should have picked a different time." Ruby's face was sad Pearl could see.

"Well, it was obviously something you needed to say so it was probably better now than later, so don't worry, I know now and that's the main thing. Has Tony told you all the arrangements are made for us to come with you?"

"Yes, he's kept me updated and, Pearl? Thank you so much, I know how hard this will be for you, but I will feel so much better knowing you are going to be there – friends to the end remember? We always used to say that at school." Ruby and Pearl laughed together at that; they had indeed said that nearly every day when they were younger.

They chatted for an hour and Ted wandered through and spoke to Ruby, "Hello, dear, how are you?" he asked Ruby.

"I'm very well, thank you, Ted, and thank you for giving Pearl the idea, it must be wonderful to speak to your family so far away." Ruby replied, marvelling at seeing Ted on the screen next to Pearl.

"Oh, it is, it is," Ted said. "I know I probably won't see them in person again, so this is the next best thing!"

Jill came over to check if they were all right and Pearl said to Ruby, "I think we should call it a day now; shall we chat again in a day or so?"

"Oh, yes, please, I'd like that so cheerio for now, my dear and I'll speak to you soon, now how do I turn thi…"

The screen went blank and Pearl sat looking at it for a minute, wondering if Ruby would appear again. She checked she had turned her Kindle off correctly and a sudden wave of sadness overcame her. When would be the last time she would hear Ruby's voice and see her smiling face – oh, it was all too difficult, this getting old lark, she thought?

Chapter 19
April 1957

"You don't think it's too cold to have the party outside, do you?" Pearl looked around the garden decorated with bunting and streamers. It was the twins' seventh birthday and they had decided the weather was warm enough to have it outside, but now there was a bit of a chill in the air, Pearl thought.

"No, it will be wonderful," puffed Ruby as she blew up another balloon. "I'm not sure about the balloons though, we might have to put them up inside if the wind picks up a bit."

"I'll see what Edward says when he gets home, but the children will be running around and they can always put a jumper on, although Susie won't want anything to hide her party dress!" Pearl said. "I'll just go in and check on the sausage rolls, Mum's coming down in a bit to help do the sandwiches and she's bringing the cake."

"Have the jellies set?" Ruby peered into the brand-new refrigerator Pearl and Edward had bought a couple of months ago. "Ooh, I love this fridge, I'm going to see if Derek will buy one. He's done quite a bit of overtime lately so we should have enough, although with the car we've now got, money is going to be a bit tight. I might have to wait a while longer."

She sighed. Derek's job as supervisor in the local mustard factory paid well, but they were both quite extravagant when it came to be spending!

"I made the jellies last night so they should be done by now." Pearl took the sausage rolls from the oven and left them to cool.

"Right, well if that's everything, I'll nip off and get my two ready." Ruby had left Tony and Jack with her mother while she helped Pearl set up. At four Tony would be in his element at the party, he adored Susie and especially Pete; he followed Pete around everywhere, who at seven seemed so much bigger and grown up. Jack had had his first birthday two months previously so he was only going to stay for an hour or so and Derek would take him home for his afternoon nap while Ruby stayed on to help.

There were about five or six other children coming who were the twins' school-friends, so it was bound to get a bit boisterous!

Eleanor was bringing Susie and Pete with her at two o'clock and hopefully Edward and her father John should be here by then as they were bringing the children's presents; they had been saving up for some time and had bought them both bicycles. They would be so excited they would want to ride them straightaway which is why they had decided the garden would be the best option.

Gwen arrived at half past twelve and they set about making the sandwiches. Pearl had already boiled the eggs and they were cooling on the side ready to go with the cress; you couldn't have a party without egg and cress sandwiches Pearl always thought. She had boiled the ham the day before, so it was just a matter of buttering the bread and assembling them.

"Where do you want the cake, dear?" Gwen said, carrying the large white box from Shepherd's the Bakers.

"I think we should put it in the dining room, it's cooler in there and the children hopefully won't go in," Pearl said peering into the box. "Ooh, Mum, that's lovely, look at the detail they've done!"

The cake was decorated in alternate pink and blue flowers and had the children's names iced across the top.

"I know, it's lovely isn't it? Now, I know you gave me the money for it, but Dad and I want to treat the children so here's your two pounds back." Gwen took the pound notes from her purse and tucked them in Pearl's apron pocket.

"Oh, Mum, no, you've bought them presents already!" Pearl said, trying to give the money back to her mother.

"No, its fine. Dad insisted, and we've only got the twins some games and odds and ends. What has Eleanor bought them?" Gwen knew how much Eleanor doted on her grandchildren and, although there wasn't really any competitiveness, Gwen always felt she wasn't giving them enough.

"Well, come and see, they're in the dining room. Bring that cake too, it looks heavy." Pearl led the way and the dining room was indeed a lot cooler than anywhere else in the house.

"Oh, my word, they are lovely," Gwen admired the train set for Pete and the lovely little dolls house for Susie. "They will be over the moon when they see them."

"Yes, I kept telling Eleanor not to spoil them too much, but you know what she's like!" Pearl would rather the twins had received these gifts for Christmas, but you couldn't reason with Eleanor. She had nothing else to spend her money on, she always said. Her husband of two years, Kenneth, was a wealthy widower with grown up children; they spent several weeks of the year having trips to Europe and Eleanor had a new lease of life. Edward and Ken got on well and he was glad to see his mother happy again.

"Oh, my goodness, it's one o'clock. Come on, Pearl, we better get a move on!" Gwen said. "They'll be here before we know it and there's still a fair bit to do."

Edward and John arrived at one fifteen and once Edward had put the bikes in the shed, he raced upstairs to change his clothes; he had been to work in the morning, and he was desperate to get out of his uniform. Bill had retired and Edward had been made station master a year ago. It was a big responsibility, but

Edward had risen to the challenge and was pleased he now had more in his pay packet to spend on his beloved wife and children.

By one forty-five everything was ready, and they sat back with a welcome cuppa waiting for the guests to arrive. They had invited the parents to stay on if they wanted to and there were a few bottles of pale ale and some stout that Edward was keen to sample. Pearl had made jugs of lemonade for the children and there was elderflower wine for the ladies which Gwen had made.

Eleanor arrived just before two o'clock with the twins; they had taken their party clothes and had changed at her house. Pete looked smart in his navy shorts and shirt with a red pullover on top. Susie was wearing her new party frock; it was pink and had an underskirt of netting which she swished about this way and that, the bodice was decorated with sequins and glinted in the sunlight.

Eleanor had put her hair in a little bun on the top of her head and her blue eyes were shining with excitement, "Hello, Gran." She kissed Gwen and skipped off to see what was in the kitchen. Pete came over and gave his grandmother a hug.

"My, you are getting a big boy now, aren't you?" Gwen said, giving him a kiss.

The twins went into the garden to greet their dad and granddad who were putting the finishing touches to the bunting and collecting some of the leaves blown about by the breeze.

"Susie? Pete?" Pearl called out, "Your guests are arriving, come and say hello."

The other children filed in and handed Susie and Pete cards and gifts "Can we open them, Mummy?" Susie asked, beyond excited.

"Yes, of course, darling." Pearl watched them open the cards and made sure they said thank you to the children and to their parents; they had received lots of presents including colouring books, crayons and some sweets.

"I think we'll put all these in the living room until later," Pearl said. "It's time to play a game!"

They played pin the tail on the donkey which Edward had nailed to the old apple tree and one of Pete's friends Richard was delighted to win his prize of a small bag of sweets.

Pearl and Gwen were just starting to set out the food on the tables outside when Ruby and Derek arrived. "Ooh, sorry we're late," Ruby said looking flustered, "Derek couldn't get the car started!

"What's the trouble with it?" Edward said. He'd been looking to get a car himself but hadn't said anything to Pearl yet.

"No idea, mate," Derek said cheerfully, "It wouldn't start so I fiddled about a bit with the engine and suddenly she turned over!" He was proud of his Ford Anglia; it wasn't new but the chap who had had it before hadn't done many miles, so it was in good nick.

"What do you think of the Morris Minor?" Edward asked, this was the car he had his eye on and was interested to know what Derek thought. Derek always had an air about him that Edward respected and the two got on well together.

"Not a bad motor that, are you looking to get one then?" Derek asked. "Best thing we ever did was getting the car, we can go anywhere in it – well, when it starts, of course!"

Ruby had gone into the kitchen to help Pearl and Gwen and left the menfolk discussing the merits of this car or that. Eleanor was happy to see her, and they chatted about the children. Eleanor took Jack from Ruby and said she would be delighted to sit with him for a bit. Ruby handed him over gratefully and took Tony outside to where the other children were playing. "It's warmed up a treat out here now," said Ruby, accepting a small glass of elderflower from Gwen. "Not too strong, is it? I can't get tipsy or I'll never get the children sorted later," she giggled.

"Best just have the one glass, then," Gwen said. "It is a bit stronger than I usually make, I think I might have overdone the sugar in this batch." She knocked back her glass and poured herself another.

"I'll have to keep an eye on Mum," Pearl said. "She's not used to drinking that much, especially in the afternoon!"

"When are we letting the twins have their you know what's?" Edward said to Pearl in a stage whisper.

"Their you know what's? Oh yes, I know what you mean now, hmm… let's wait until they've eaten then we are going to play musical chairs, and after that we can tidy the tables and chairs away and they can have the garden path to go up down on," Pearl said, calling all the children to sit at the little tables and have some sandwiches. She poured lemonade for them all then sipped at her own glass of elderflower wine. "My goodness, this is strong!" She grimaced as the alcohol hit her.

"Well, if you're having that, I'm opening a pale ale." Edward set off and rounded up the one or two dads who had stayed and they were soon sharing a pint and chatting.

The afternoon went really well, and they made sure each child had won something small in the games; the last game was pass the parcel with Tony thrilled to win the main prize of a packet of chalks. The adults cleared the garden for the big surprise.

Edward called Susie and Pete over to the shed and opened the door. The children's faces were beaming when they saw the shiny, new bicycles in there; a red one for Susie and a blue one for Pete, and soon they were off riding round the children and generously letting the other children take turns.

Eleanor had helped Pearl and Ruby put the candles on the cake as Gwen was nodding off in a deckchair after having succumbed to the elderflower wine. "She'll have a headache later," said John. "Are there any sausage rolls left? I doubt I'll get any supper tonight with the state of her," he chuckled.

"Yes, Dad, there's loads left. I'll put you some by and you can take them with you. There's cake too, look, there should be enough left." Pearl called Edward to light the candles and Ruby called in the children. They all sang Happy Birthday – except Gwen who by now was snoring softly in the garden – and they cheered when Susie and Pete blew all the candles out in one go!

"Now, if you go into the dining room, there's one more surprise each!" said Pearl, winking at Eleanor. The twins ran off and they could hear excited squeals as they revealed the train set and dolls house.

The children all played happily for another half hour, then the adults decided it was time to leave. Pearl cut them all slices of cake to take home wrapped in birthday napkins. Derek had taken Jack home earlier and Tony was playing trains with Pete so Ruby helped Pearl to clear up. After a strong coffee, Gwen had managed to get home with John holding her arm firmly in case she toppled over, a bag of food in his other hand for his supper.

"Are you okay to walk home, Ruby? Or do you want to walk with me when I take Mum home?" Edward said. "I know it's a bit of a detour, but it won't take too long."

"If you're sure you don't mind?" Ruby said. It was getting late and, although the nights were lighter for longer, she still preferred to have Edward with her.

"No trouble at all. Mum's just getting her coat, then we're ready. Leave the washing up, love," he said to Pearl. "I'll give you a hand when I get back, you look exhausted."

"There's only these last few bits to do. I tell you what, I'll do these, and you can help bath the children; they're a bit grubby from being in the garden all afternoon and they can't get into bed with their feet covered in muck!" Pearl chuckled.

"It's a deal, I'll be as quick as I can." He kissed Pearl goodbye and she embraced Eleanor and thanked her for her help. Pearl and Ruby embraced warmly, and Pearl thanked her again for her help, too.

"I was glad to help, it's what friends are for," Ruby said, smiling at Pearl's tired face. "Friends to the end remember!"

Pearl smiled as she closed the door and finished the tidying up. It had been a good day and the children were playing quietly, but she could tell they were tired and soon they would be bickering. She hoped Edward wouldn't be too long, she was dead on her feet!

Later that same year in the summer holidays, after Edward had swallowed his pride for the sake of his family and accepted the generous loan from Ken to buy a car with very reasonable repayments, the two families set off for the day to the coast. Edward loaded up the Morris Minor with all the paraphernalia they would need and drove round to Ruby and Derek's house. They too were just finishing getting everything packed away.

Pearl and Ruby had organised sandwiches and they were going to treat the children to some chips when they got there. Eleanor had given all the children, including Tony and baby Jack, a sixpence each for an ice cream so they were excited to be off to Hunstanton.

The sun shone all day and it was idyllic. They paddled in the sea and built sandcastles. They thoroughly enjoyed their chips – why did they always taste so much better at the coast?

The children slept all the way home, Edward and Pearl chatted quietly and Pearl thought her life couldn't get any better!

Chapter 20
June 2018

After her chat with Ruby, Pearl suddenly was feeling low. It was probably like a sugar rush, she thought, having been so excited to speak to Ruby then coming down from a high once she had clicked off. She wondered how Ruby was feeling. Although she was very glad to have spoken with her, she wondered how much longer she could keep doing it – well, she knew she only had until the end of August, obviously, but there were still several weeks to go and she was finding it hard going talking to Ruby knowing their time together was coming to an end.

She desperately wanted to talk about it to someone, but to whom? She wasn't sure she should speak to Jill as she wasn't sure what Jill would say; as understanding as she was, she was still in the business of caring for people! Susie wasn't coming again for a few days. She could ring her, and she would come over; Pearl knew Susie would drop everything for her, but it wasn't fair, Susie had enough to get on with as it was without running around after a silly old fool.

She told herself she would feel better in the morning and resolved to keep her thoughts to herself.

She made her way to the dining room where a lively discussion about Brexit was taking place over dinner. Pearl didn't join in, she had no time for politics, but it was a welcome distraction to hear the others debating the pros and cons of the subject.

A bit later she sat with Ted and Betty and watched a drama on the television, but halfway through she could feel her eyelids drooping. "I think I'm going to retire to bed," she told them.

"Oh, but this is the best bit, they start to reveal who's likely to be the killer!" Ted said. "We don't find out who it is until the end of the programme, but, my moneys on that shifty bugger in the black jacket. Look, there he is now, the low life – Oh! Bugger, he's just been shot!"

Pearl laughed and said she would leave them to solve the mystery. Jill helped her get ready for bed as usual. "You seem a bit quiet tonight, Pearl, everything all right? You had a lovely chat with Ruby earlier, didn't you?"

"Oh, it was marvellous, Jill," Pearl said, smiling at her. "It was so good to see her while talking to her at the same time!"

"Technology is a wonderful thing," Jill said, "Though there are times when it's not so good. Having to get my teenagers to tear themselves away from Facebook or Instagram is a nightmare!" She plumped Pearl's pillows as she looked at her blankly. "They are social media platforms."

"I'm none the wiser." Pearl was confused by Jill now.

"Ha, ha. Well, Facebook is an interactive site where people put pictures and videos and keep in touch with other people, they are friends with and Instagram is where people share photos," Jill explained.

"Oh, so you mean a bit like where I was talking to Ruby earlier on the Kindle?" Pearl asked.

"Yes, very similar to that, love. Now are you sure you're, all right?" Jill looked at Pearl and carried on. "Are you worrying about Ruby and her trip to Switzerland?" she asked gently.

Pearl shot upright, aghast. "How on earth did you know about that? I didn't think anyone here knew about it!"

"Well, Pearl, we do talk to each other in the homes you know? High End have spoken to us here and of course your daughter and son-in-law have explained about you taking the trip too, so yes, I know all about what's going on." Jill sat on the chair next to Pearl's bed "If there is anything you need to talk about, please don't bottle it up. You know you can talk to me, we don't necessarily advocate self-euthanasia, but we do understand the reasoning behind it and in the past we had a chap in here in a very similar situation to your friend and he decided it was the only way that would work for him."

Pearl was so relieved Jill was aware of all that was going on. Of course, she would, she chided herself, how on earth did she think she was going to go off to Switzerland without anyone noticing. I am a bloody old fool, she thought – not for the first time that day!

"So?" said Jill, "What's on your mind?"

Pearl wasn't sure how to start then it all came out in a rush. "I'm not really sure how I feel about it. I know it was a complete shock when Ruby first told me."

"That was why you looked so poorly at your party," Jill cut in, she hadn't been told exactly when Pearl was given the news, but she suspected it was at the party.

"Yes, she told me that afternoon and I was at a complete loss as to what to say to her. I couldn't believe Ruby would do something like that, but then I started to think about it, and she was always more forthcoming than me, more, what's the word? Daring, I suppose, so it made sense she would consider it." Pearl took a deep breath. "I could see why she wanted to go, she's obviously in some considerable pain with her problems and I wanted to give her my blessing. I thought there was no need to make it more difficult for her, but now, now I think how selfish she's being!" Pearl's voice was wavering slightly. "That makes me such a bad person to think like that, doesn't it? Because Ruby is the least selfish person I know, and I know for her it's the best thing to do, but all I can think about is what about me? What about her two lovely sons and their families? How are we all supposed to just say 'Okay, bye, Ruby, nice knowing you' and go on with our lives as if nothing has happened? And that makes me the selfish one!" Pearl was so upset by her thoughts; Jill gave her some water to sip.

"What you are feeling, Pearl, is perfectly understandable," Jill said. "It's called 'survivor guilt'. People get it when they walk away from an accident that has claimed a life or lives. There have been people walk away from plane crashes that others have died in and they can't believe why they haven't died and so they feel guilty. Of course, you are going to think 'what about me?' You have spent most of your lives together and it's hard to imagine how you are going to cope once one of you is gone, but you can survive, Pearl, you have managed to carry on without Edward, haven't you?"

"Well, yes, oh that was hard, but I didn't know he was dying, do you see? He went to the doctors as he was feeling a bit under the weather, the doctor prescribed him some tablets and he went up to the hospital for tests. When the results came back, they whisked him in and within a few days he was gone – just like that!" Pearl snapped her fingers. "It was cancer, and at least he didn't suffer for which I'm glad."

"Well, exactly," Jill said gently, "And that's what it will be like for Ruby. She won't suffer anymore. You know her biggest fear is not knowing anyone if her dementia gets worse – which, unfortunately, it probably will do and quickly. Can you imagine how hard that will be for you when you talk to her and she doesn't know who you are? I think that's harder than not having her here at all, don't you?"

"So, you're saying she's actually being selfless, isn't she? She's thinking of us more than she is herself," Pearl said thoughtfully.

"Well, in a way, yes she is. Obviously, she's thinking about her life and the way it is her for at the moment, constantly in pain and taking tablets which only relieve some of the pain, it's not really making her better is it?" Jill said gently. She could see the turmoil Pearl was in. "I think she feels she's had a good life and this way it will end the way she wants, and everyone will remember the good things about her life and not be thinking how bad it was for her at the end."

"Yes, I see what you are saying, and that is Ruby to a T. She always put everyone first before she thought of how it might affect her; such a dear friend, I've been so lucky to have her in my life – friends to the end!" Pearl smiled. "That was what we always used to say when we were growing up and that's what we'll be, right to the end!"

"So, do you feel any better about it all now? As I said, if ever you want to chat, I'm here and Margaret obviously knows too, so if I'm not around you can always speak to her. You're not alone in this, Pearl, we are all here for you and for Ruby too." Jill got up and straightened the duvet for Pearl. "Do you think you can sleep now, dear?"

"Yes, thank you, Jill. I'll be fine, thank you for listening and explaining things to me." Pearl was feeling as if a burden had been lifted from her shoulders and she thought she would sleep better tonight.

Jill left the night light and when she went to check on Pearl an hour later, she was fast asleep.

Chapter 21
February 1963

"Well, I think it's a bloody brilliant idea, but can we all afford it?" Ruby, Derek and the boys were at Pearl and Edward's for tea. After they had eaten, they sat chatting round the dining table. The children were watching the television in the other room; it was a fairly new acquisition for Pearl and Edward, it was on hire purchase and Pearl only allowed the children a certain amount of time on it after they had done their homework – not that it was on for long anyway!

"Don't swear, dear," Pearl said to Edward. "But yes, can we all afford to go to Spain for a week? What about passports and things? How much will it all cost?"

"Well, it's certainly not cheap!" Derek said telling them the cost. "But the passports we get last for a year and the children go on ours so there's only us four to get. We book it through what's called a package holiday, so everything's taken care of. They arrange the transport to the hotel and everything. We will be full board, so all the food is sorted too, just the drinks to pay for," Derek explained, winking at Edward as he mentioned the drinks.

"Ooh, come on, Pearl, it'll be fab!" Ruby was excited by the thought of going on an aeroplane to Spain. It sounded so exotic and she had been talking of nothing else for days now. She had gone back to work as soon as Jack was old enough and they had some money to spend.

"Can we do it, Edward?" Pearl looked at her husband. She knew that they did have a bit put by; Edward was still the station master at the railway, and he was earning good money. She had returned to work when the children were smaller, and it was a big help having her pay packet each week. She was hoping to get that new sofa she had her eye on, but she supposed the one they had would do for another year.

"I think we might. I'll have to look at the finances tonight, but it sounds like we might be able to just about afford it." Edward smiled at the others and thought they would make it work. It would be wonderful to take his darling wife and children on a week's holiday to Spain of all places. He could see the envious faces of the chaps at work when he told them his news.

"Yippee!" Ruby whooped, dancing around with Pearl. "We're all going on a summer holiday!" she sang as they twirled about the kitchen.

"Ssh!" Pearl said. "I don't want the children to know until it's booked and paid for. They would be so disappointed if it doesn't come off."

"Ooh, sorry. It's just so exciting and think of the kids' faces when they get on the plane!" Ruby said.

"Yes, well, I'm not sure I'm too keen on that bit myself!" Edward said warily. "Are they safe?" he looked to Derek.

"Ha, ha, yes, old boy, perfectly safe. In fact, it's safer than crossing the road these days!" Derek laughed; he was pleased the others were going. They had had days at the coast and even had a caravan trip for a week to the seaside, but this felt like a real holiday. He was looking forward to it and apparently you didn't need to speak the lingo either; they knew English over there!

"What's the money over there?" Pearl asked, "Is it the potato or something?"

Ruby burst out laughing. "It's the Spanish *Peseta*, silly! Although I think we will now rename it the Potato!"

"Ah, that's it; I knew it was something like that!" Pearl laughed along with the others. "We'll have to go shopping though, Ruby. I can't wear that tatty old swimming costume I've got; I've had it for years and it's pretty threadbare now. Oh, and the twins will need new bathing suits too and sandals!" She looked stricken as she thought how much more it was going to cost them to kit them all out for a week!

"Now, darling, don't worry about that. It's the twins' birthday coming up; I'll have a word with Mum and see if she wants to buy them the togs they need instead of a toy or whatever. How does that sound?" Edward knew his mother would gladly pay for the whole holiday, but his pride wasn't going to allow that, but for the children. Well, that was different; he had made all the repayments to Ken for the car loan, so his money was his own again.

"Yes, my mum and dad said something similar," Derek agreed. "So, are we all in then? Shall I go down and book it?"

"Well, let me check our finances and I'll let you know tomorrow, if that's okay? Then yes, book it and let's go!" With that he grabbed Pearl where she had just sat down and danced her round the kitchen.

"Ha, ha, Edward! Put me down!" Pearl was giggling along with the others as they carried on making plans until it was time for Ruby and Derek to take the boys home for a bath and bed.

Chapter 22
June 1963

The suitcases were finally packed, and they were all ready to leave. The twins were beyond excited, and Susie was jumping up and down with expectation; she had lots of lovely new clothes to wear and a beautiful pink swimming costume her Nana Eleanor had bought for her. She had always loved new outfits, although Pete didn't seem to mind wearing the same old stuff day in day out. Even Pete was excited, though he was looking forward to sitting on the plane and hearing the engines roar as they took off. As Pete was nearly thirteen, they had told him he was sitting next to Jack, so he was hoping Jack didn't wee himself if it got frightening!

Grandma Gwen had given them a pound note each for spending money and they had given it to their dad to look after, with the stern reminder he wasn't allowed to spend it!

They arrived at the airport in plenty of time and checked the luggage in; the children were fascinated to see it disappear and Jack wanted to know how it would get to their hotel.

They wandered around and stopped for a cup of tea. The prices were astronomical, but Edward had decided he wasn't going to worry too much about money this week. If they wanted it, well, then they would have it – within reason, he added.

Soon it was time to board the plane and they all marvelled at how lovely it was. The air hostess, who Susie thought very glamorous in her uniform, brought them all barley sugar sweets for take-off as their ears might pop, she explained. Luckily for Pete, Jack didn't wet himself, but he did grab his hand as the engines roared loudly just as they lifted off the ground!

They arrived at their hotel later that evening all feeling weary and, once they were settled in their rooms, decided an early night would be best. They would be fresh for their first full day of their holiday in the morning. They all slept like tops and were ready for their breakfasts the next day.

"Ah, this is the life," Derek said, sipping his beer while the children splashed and swam in the swimming pool. "How's your stomach now, mate?" he asked Edward who was looking a bit grey still. They had been there two days and Edward had succumbed to the inevitable holiday tummy!

"I'm not too bad today, thanks. I've kept my breakfast down at any rate, so I think I'm on the mend," Edward replied. He was determined not to let anything spoil this week. It had cost him a king's ransom and would probably take him the best part of a year to pay back the money he had borrowed from their nest egg, but it was worth it to see Susie and Pete already turning as brown as berries and having fun. He looked over to where Pearl and Ruby were lying on their sun beds looking very glamorous, he thought, in their new bathing suits.

"This is the best holiday I've ever had!" Ruby declared as she chinked glasses with Pearl. They had learned quite quickly that drinking in the heat of the day wasn't a good idea, so they stuck to lemonade by the pool and on the beach "I'm so glad we came, even if it's expensive aren't you, Pearl?"

"Yes, it's marvellous, I can't get over how blue the sea is, so different to Wells or Hunstanton!" She laughed. "The children all seem to be having a great time, too. They can all swim like fish now and we've only been here two days! Look how brown your Tony is, whatever colour will he be by the end of the week?"

"I know!" said Ruby. "I keep putting on the suntan lotion but he's in and out of the water so much it washes off. He doesn't look like he's going to burn though. How's Susie's shoulders now?"

"Much better now. The lady on reception told me what to buy and it seems to be doing the trick. She's so fair and the sun is hotter than it is home that's for sure!" Pearl stretched out her shapely legs and admired the golden glow she was getting on them.

The following day they went on a trip organised by the hotel to see some of the local crafts and museums. It was exhausting wandering around in the heat even though they were all wearing shorts; they were glad to be back in the hotel and able to wash off all the dust.

All too soon it was their last evening; they had a lovely meal and the hotel put on a show with Spanish dancers, the guests were invited up and they all danced the night away.

The following morning Derek wished he hadn't had so much wine the night before; he wasn't feeling the best! He hoped there was no turbulence on the flight home and vowed to make sure there was a sick bag in the front pocket of his seat – just in case!

All the children were excited at the thought of going on a plane again, even if it was to take them home. Susie had enjoyed the holiday so much – apart from her sore shoulders and she couldn't wait to tell her friends all about it; she was the first one in her little group to go abroad.

Pearl and Ruby sat together on the plane, with Susie sitting by the window. "What a lovely time we have had," Pearl said, "Thank you so much for talking us into it, sweetheart." She looked at Ruby fondly.

"No, thank you, Pearl!" Ruby said. "You, Edward and the twins have made it the best time ever. I'll never forget this. Maybe, once we've all saved up enough, we can do it again?"

"I'd love to, but it might take a few years, and I really do want to get that new sofa I was telling you about," Pearl said wistfully. "I'll have to scrub up the old one for this year though and maybe see if it's still there in the new year!"

Chapter 23
June 2018

Ruby was thrilled she had been able to talk to Pearl earlier that day. She had loved seeing her old friend's face on the little screen. Oh, it wasn't as good as actually sitting with her, but it was the next best thing and she hoped they would do it again soon. Now she had so little time left she found herself reminiscing about all the things they had done together.

She remembered when they all went to Spain on holiday together. It was the first time any of them had been out of the British Isles and it was certainly an eye opener. They vowed to go again, and they did several years later, without the children though as they were grown up and working by the time, they could all afford to go again. She remembered fondly Edgar having a dodgy tummy almost immediately they arrived; no not Edgar! What was his name?

Edmund, that was it! He hadn't been well for the first two days but carried on determined to have a good time. Derek was fine, though he had had plenty to drink and swam with the childr... Hang on, it wasn't Edmund either, was it?

'Oh, lord,' she thought, 'I can't remember my oldest and best friend's husband's name!' She sat trying not to think of anything and suddenly it came to her. EDWARD! A cold sweat had enveloped her as she realised this was the start. How soon would it be before she couldn't remember Pearl's name or, heaven forbid, her beloved boys?

She tried to calm herself down and took several deep breaths. She repeated, 'You will be all right, not long to go now' like a mantra until she felt a little better. She had a flash of inspiration and reached for her writing pad; she would write down everyone's names and hopefully that would help her remember.

Her parents, *Alf* and *Mavis*. Luckily, she had no siblings; she had always wanted a sister but now she was glad as it was just one more name to remember. 'Now, let's see, there's *Tony* and *Jeannie* of course and their children *Tom* (married to Karen), *Oliver* their son (married to Megan and they had Will with the new baby imminent). Oh, this is going really well,' she thought, 'I'm remembering all these names straightaway.' She was feeling more like her old self again now and confidently continued to jot the names down; her darling *Jack* and *Maria*; their two girls *Kirsty* (engaged to Jordan) and *Maddie* (whose boyfriend was Matt).

So far, so good, she was so pleased with herself. She heard the dining room start to get busy as the residents started to make their way into lunch and Mandy came in just then to help her up and make her way in to join the others. She tucked her writing pad in the drawer and decided to continue a bit later.

After her lunch she was delighted to see Jack making his way over to where she was sitting in the day room. The patio doors were open, and it was lovely to sit and enjoy the sunshine streaming in. There were some steps leading out to the garden and a ramp for the wheelchairs, but she preferred to sit by the doors as it was difficult to manage either unless she went in one of the chairs; she was trying to hold off from that as long as possible, although she had agreed to the wheelchair assistance for the airport – she would be dead before she got on the plane if she had to walk all that way!

Airports seemed to go on forever and when Tony and Jack had taken her to Switzerland in March, she was glad of the ease it brought her.

"Hello, my love, what brings you here?" She beamed up at her youngest son. At sixty-three Jack had more grey in his hair, but, like his brother, it suited him – distinguished, her dad always used to say!

"Hi, Mum, I thought I'd pop in and see my favourite girl!" Jack kissed his mother and breathed in her scent, trying to capture it as a memory. "How are you? How was the Kindle experiment with Pearl? A success?"

"Oh, yes, it was wonderful. Just to see her face and talk to her, you know?" Ruby smiled. "It did me the power of good. We chatted for about an hour and Ted came in and said 'hello' too!"

"Excellent!" Jack said, "When are you doing it again?"

"I think a bit later this week or early next week. Maybe you or Tony could ring Susie and set it up again for us, darling, if you don't mind?" Ruby said hopefully.

"Anytime you like, Mum. Shall we say in two days' time? You might as well get as many chats in as you can before... er... before...," he tailed off unable to finish the sentence.

"I know, dear, I know, and I've been thinking the same thing, so don't worry." Ruby helped him out. "I know how hard this is for you, my love, but I need to count on your support and your brother's too."

"We do support you, Mum, both of us, one hundred percent. I'm sorry, sometimes it just hits me like a tidal wave, and I want you to live forever!" Jack laughed softly.

"Ha, ha, now can you imagine that. Unfortunately, darling, there is no fountain of eternal youth and we all have to go at some point. This way I get to be in control, you do understand, don't you?" she asked him imploringly, looking at his face and remembering every line and crease, imprinting it onto her memory, just as Jack had done when he had first arrived.

Jack nodded and, taking his mother's hand, they both sat in silence as they enjoyed their close bond.

"So," Ruby broke the silence. The look on Jack's face was heart-breaking and she hated herself for what she was doing to them, but she knew it was the kindest thing and, in a way, the best lasting gift she could ever give them. They can't see it now, she thought, but in years to come they'll be thankful, of that she was sure.

"So," she said again. "How exciting and unexpected for Milly to have her baby so early, wasn't it? I believe its Megan's baby party – is that what they call it? Next week isn't it? Poor Milly didn't get to have hers with the baby arriving so quickly." She had forgotten the baby's name but everyone just said 'baby' to begin with so she didn't think Jack would comment on it.

"Yes, that's right, I think they call it a baby shower though," Jack replied, relieved to be on a safer topic – although when you think about it, it's either life or death, that's what it comes down to, he thought morosely. He mentally shook himself; this wasn't why he visited. He certainly didn't want to upset his mum. He was just desperate to make as many memories and spend as much time as he could with her; he wasn't getting any younger either and he was terrified he would forget her face and her unique scent.

He took a breath and continued the conversation keeping it light and chatty for his mum. "They are all besotted with Olivia, she is gorgeous."

'Ah, that's her name.' Ruby made a mental note to add that in her writing pad later!

"Pearl is going to show me some pictures the next time we chat as Susie is going to come over and she has them on her phone or something. How does the phone know you are taking a picture, dear? Does it ring them up at the same time or something?" She remembered the old Bakelite telephones they had had at work and in later years every household had a telephone, but as far as she was aware none of them were able to take pictures – you had to have a camera for that, didn't you?

"Ha, ha, the mobile phones nowadays all have built in cameras, Mum, so you go to the right bit and it opens up the camera. Then you just point and shoot the same way you and Dad did with a Kodak!" He had to admit he was amazed by the how fast the technology had progressed, he could remember the old phones – his favourite was the trim phone with its unique trilling ring tone; he and his mates practised for hours trying to perfect the sound.

"Ah, right, I see," said Ruby, none the wiser, but it didn't really matter. "Well, they will be lovely I'm sure."

"Maria said she will come in and sit with you one afternoon this week. I'm not sure of the day, but she'll sort something out," Jack said. He would visit every day in the next few weeks, he vowed. He looked at his mother and was struck by how frail she was looking nowadays, but it also occurred to him that she was the strongest person he had ever known!

"Oh, that will be lovely," Ruby said. "You know, when you first started to go out with Maria, I wasn't sure she was the right girl for you, but it didn't take long to see that behind that slightly frosty exterior, she had a heart of gold and was full of warmth and Dad loved her too."

It was over thirty years now since they had met and married and Jack still thought he was punching above his weight with Maria; he too had thought she was too stuck up for the likes of him, but she was actually quite shy underneath it all. He had met her at a party and was instantly attracted to her – along with the hundred or so other blokes there, but to his surprise she had been content to chat with him and they had chatted on long into the night.

The following morning, he lay in his bed and couldn't stop thinking about her. He was about to hop in the shower when his phone rang – it was Maria! She said how great the party was – he couldn't remember anything about it all – and asked him if he wanted to meet up for a coffee? He was gobsmacked, to say the least! He had thought it was just a one-off meeting as she was model and everything, but no, she had seen something she liked obviously.

Now at sixty, she was still as beautiful as she once was, and Jack was more in love with her than ever – if that was possible!

He could see Ruby was tiring and, as reluctant as he was to go, he left her to take an afternoon nap, promising to come and see her again very soon.

"It's lovely to see you, darling, thank you so much for coming over." Ruby was indeed getting tired. She needed to take one of the myriad of pills she took every day and she would nap for a couple of hours to ease some of the pain in her joints.

After Jack had left, she made her way stiffly back to her room, and just before she nodded off, she jotted down *Olivia* in her writing pad.

Chapter 24
April 1968

Susie woke up on the Saturday morning wondering what was so special about today; she didn't have the dentist or doctor's, did she? So, what was it – Oh, my god! She jumped out of bed – of course! Today was the day of the party, she and Pete had turned eighteen the day before and they were having a joint party – if she was honest, she probably would have preferred to have had her own party without Pete's friends; some of them were distinctly odd, but her parents had said it would be less expensive this way and as they were paying for everything she couldn't really disagree, besides some of Pete's friends were quite cute so it would be great, she was sure.

She looked at her dress hanging on the outside of the wardrobe, she had been saving for ages for the black and white checkerboard mini dress from her Saturday job at Woolworths and she knew it looked fantastic on her. Her Nana Eleanor had given her some birthday money and she had bought some knee-high white boots to go with it. Her hair was styled in a pixie cut which went so well with her elfin features, everyone had told her.

Pete was also looking forward to the party later on. A lot of Susie's friends were stunners and he had his eye on one or two! He too had been given birthday money from Nana Eleanor, but he hadn't bothered wasting it on clothes; he'd bought some new fishing gear – much better!

The party was being held in the local pub; their dad had booked the back room and their mum, Grandma Gwen and Auntie Ruby would do the food. Dad and Uncle Derek were sorting out the beer, so it would be a good night, he thought. He had invited several of his mates from college and he had bumped into a friend he hadn't seen for ages – Dan Finch. He was a good bloke and Pete had asked him to come along if he wasn't doing anything. Dan had said he was home for a few weeks, and he would certainly be there; it would be good to catch up with the other lads they knew.

Pearl and Ruby were in the city centre shopping for dresses to wear that evening. "I can't believe your two are eighteen! Where has the time gone?" Ruby said when they stopped to have a cup of tea.

Pearl's feet were killing her, and she was glad to sit down for ten minutes. "I know!" she said, "The years just fly by, don't they? Edward was only saying the other day he was nearly forty-two, way past middle age!"

"Well, we are almost forty, so I suppose it's all downhill from now on, girl!" Ruby laughed. "The boys are so looking forward to the party tonight. Tony still looks up to Pete, even after all these years. I've told them they can't stay to the end though, especially Jack, he's only thirteen and I'd rather get him home before the party gets too loud."

"Well, hopefully Mum won't have made any elderflower wine!" Pearl and Ruby almost choked on their tea when they remembered Gwen from the twins' seventh birthday party.

"Ha, ha! Yes, she did get through it, didn't she?" Ruby said. "She'll probably stick to Babycham tonight."

"She's always liked a drink though," Pearl said. "I used to worry about her and drinking, but she said it was only high days and holidays and during the week she didn't touch a drop. I used to watch her when I went around and, to be honest, she never had anything while I was there or when the twins were with her, so I'm sure she was telling the truth and Dad would have sorted her out if she did anyway." Pearl drained her cup and said, "Right, let's get back to it, if I don't find something in the next hour I'm giving up and wearing something I've already got!"

"Ah, come on, don't give up, the perfect dresses are just waiting for us, you'll see!" Ruby steered her friend into one of the more expensive shops and to Pearl's delight they both found exactly what they were looking for.

"It's not too short, is it?" Pearl loved the dress she was wearing – a paisley lemon and blue shift with a tie belt although it was tiny bit too mini for her taste. She checked the back in the mirror and liked the way her legs looked in it.

"Don't be daft! It looks fabulous on you and you know it! You'll give Susie's friends a run for their money looking like that and Edward? Well, Edward will fall even more madly in love with you!" Ruby was envious of her friend's slim figure, although she thought she didn't scrub up too bad herself and the dress she had chosen fitted her like a glove. Hers was a dusky pink and she had seen something similar worn by Twiggy in a magazine the other week; the colour suited her, and she knew Derek would love it.

"Come on, let's get them." Pearl made her mind up and she couldn't face tramping round any more shops. They still had to get the food ready for later, although if she knew her mum, she had been up baking since dawn probably!

"I can't believe how much we have just spent on two blooming dresses!" Pearl grumbled as they made their way home.

"Ah, it's only money," said Ruby, "And, besides, we look fabulous in them, so it's money well spent in my book and Derek said I was to get what I liked and not worry about the price."

"Yes, I know, Edward said more or less the same. I just don't like spending too much of his money on me, although I did pay half." Pearl reconciled the cost to herself and they walked home swinging their bags, excitedly talking about later.

"Ooh, Mum, that is so pretty." Susie admired Pearl's dress as she took it out of the bag and showed her. "That will go perfectly with your cream shoes, are you going to wear them?"

"Yes, I thought they would do, after spending all that on the dress I couldn't really justify new shoes as well and besides, my feet will only ache later if I haven't worn them in," Pearl said, hanging the dress up in her bedroom and poking about in the wardrobe for the shoes.

"Do they look all right? They look a bit dusty, don't they?" Pearl was a bit dubious now, but she didn't have time to go back to the shops this afternoon.

"Here, give them to me. I'll give them a wipe over and see what they look like. I'm sure they'll be fine and with the lights out later it will be okay, and you know Dad likes to dance so he'll no doubt be waltzing you around and you'll be glad of your comfy shoes then – you'll have to tell him not to embarrass me in front of my friends though with his dancing!" Susie said in mock horror.

"Ah, thank you, darling, that will be great. I can get on and help Mum with the food, oh, and I can't do anything about your Dad's dancing – as soon as the music starts, he's off!" Pearl laughed and thought fondly of her husband who still liked to jive to everything regardless of the beat of the music.

She went down to help Gwen with the food. Ruby was coming over in an hour to help then she was going to get ready at Pearl's and they would all leave together.

"Oh, Mum, you've got on so well." Gwen had near enough finished all the cooking; it was just the sandwiches and things to be made up at the last minute. Eleanor had bought the cake and it was already at the pub as it was easier getting it delivered there and they said they would keep it in the kitchen out the back where it would be cooler.

"Here, sit yourself down and I'll make you a cuppa." Pearl looked at her mother. At sixty-two Gwen was looking her age and she was glad to get the weight off and sit down.

"Thanks, darling, I may have overdone it a bit, but I wanted to make sure most of it was done before you got back." She had made several batches of sausage rolls; she had covered grapefruits with tin foil and stuck cocktail sticks laden with cubes of cheese, pineapple and tiny pearl onions; there were three types of quiche and a couple of pork pies she had made!

"I think we probably have enough here to feed an army and that's without the sandwiches and crisps yet to do!" Pearl was amazed at how much was ready. "I'll let the sausage rolls cool down a bit down, then start getting them packed into the boxes and Edward can run them over the pub in a bit. Me and Ruby will lay it all out, so you haven't any more to do except get ready and enjoy yourself." She hugged her mother and poured the tea.

Edward's eyebrows rose when he saw how short Susie's dress was and was about to say something, but a warning glance from Pearl made him shut his mouth and smile grimly. At least he would be at the party, he thought, and he could keep an eye on those boys – he knew what they were like, after all he was young once – albeit a long time ago now!

He was so proud of both of his children and wanted them to have a brilliant time tonight. He had put some money behind the bar and so the first few drinks were on him. He looked around the back room in the pub and thought the girls had done a lovely job decorating it. It could look a bit gloomy in the daylight, but with fairy lights everywhere and balloons it was transformed.

He joined Derek and Pearl's dad John for a beer at the bar. He was only having the one for now as he was going to run over and pick up his mother and Ken. They were only going to drop in for an hour or so as the noise would be too much, his mother said, at seventy-three she was getting too old for the loud music of today and much preferred to stay in with a documentary on the television. Ken was nearly eighty and he didn't like driving in the dark anymore as his eyesight wasn't too good with the headlights flashing, so Edward had offered to pick them up and run them home.

Susie and Pete were delighted their friends had all turned up and they put their cards and gifts on a side table to be opened later. Pete was especially pleased a couple of the old boys he went fishing with had turned up. They had taken Pete under their wing when he first joined the Wensum Fishing Club and he introduced them to his Granddad John. One of them knew John to say hello to and they were soon engrossed in conversation near the bar.

The party was in full swing and everyone was enjoying themselves. Edward had taken his mother and Ken home at nine thirty p.m. and was now on his third pint of the evening. He watched the young people all swaying about to the music and decided to join them. Susie was horrified, but soon was laughing as all her friends were copying her dad and they all danced along.

Dan had arrived later than he wanted, and he almost didn't turn up at all; his favourite shirt wasn't clean and ironed – his fault for not putting it in the wash basket! His mother came to the rescue and quickly rinsed it through, ironed it while it was still wet and hung it up near the fireplace to dry. It was nearly ten p.m. by the time he got there, and the collar was still a bit damp, but he was here and ready for a pint!

He chatted to a couple of lads he knew and turned from the bar to watch the dancing, keeping an eye out for Pete. He saw the stunning blonde in the black and white mini dress dancing and laughing with her friends and was instantly smitten. Where was Pete, he thought, he might know her, and he can introduce me!

Susie had stopped to catch her breath and as she was making her way over to her seat, she could feel someone's eyes watching her. She looked around but couldn't see who it was. She shrugged it off and sat down next to her mum who was chatting with Ruby and Grandma Gwen. "How are you enjoying retirement then, Gwen?" Ruby said. "Is it difficult now John's home all day as well, or are you getting on all right?" she asked.

"Well, it's not too bad most of the time. I usually try and get the shopping done and the housework or whatever out of the way in the mornings. John is painting the back bedroom at the moment so we're out of each other's hair. In the afternoons he gets a bit bored though and keeps saying he might take up a hobby. I don't know what he wants to do though, so we'll see." Gwen seemed to be busier than ever now she wasn't working. She had always like baking and was helping out at the local W.I. as well so it was all right for her. She was a little worried about John though, wondering what he was going to do once he had finished the decorating, but she was watching him now talking to those old boys who went fishing so maybe he could take that up and she knew Pete would be pleased if his granddad came along and joined in.

"Hello, love," Pearl said to Susie as she sat down and picked up her drink, "Are you enjoying yourself?"

"It's fab, Mum, thank you. All the girls are saying how lovely the food is, Grandma Gwen, so thank you too!" Susie beamed at them.

"Looks like Pete's friends are enjoying it too." Ruby peered across the room to the tables. "Who is that lad there?"

"Which one?" Pearl said. "The one with the blue shirt? I'm not sure, although he is familiar. One of Pete's mates? Unless you know him, Susie?"

Susie looked over to where her mum was pointing and saw who she meant, "No idea, Mum, I don't recognise him. He must be one of Pete's lot."

"Well, he looks delicious!" Ruby said flirtatiously. "Ooh, hello, darling," she said as Derek came over and whisked her onto the dance floor. They were playing some of the slower dances now, Edward soon came over and claimed Pearl.

"No one you fancy a smooch with, dear?" Gwen said to Susie. "Pete's found someone; I see." They looked over and Pete was slow dancing with Susie's friend Isobel.

"Yes, she's a nice girl and she's always liked Pe... Oh sorry!" Susie was cut off by the young man in the blue shirt standing in front of her.

"Dance?" he said, taking her hand before she could reply. He led Susie onto the dance floor, and he held her so close she could feel his heart beating through his shirt. He had checked with Pete who she was and was astounded when he said it was his sister! He knew he had a twin but wasn't imagining anything as stunning as Susie He'd asked Pete if he minded if he asked her to dance and Pete had laughed and said to go over and if Susie didn't want to dance, she would soon let him know.

Two years later they were married, and Caroline was on the way – Susie always had very happy memories of her eighteenth birthday party!

Chapter 25
June 2018

"Well! What a to do! It's a bugger and that's no mistake!" Ted was muttering to himself as he passed Pearl's room. "I don't know what to do about it, it's buggered me that has." He was shaking his head as he went to his room.

What on earth is the old fool muttering on about now? Pearl thought, as she waited for Jill to come in and help her get dressed ready for the day. Half an hour later and Jill still hadn't appeared; Pearl decided she could maybe manage to get up by herself but thought better of it when she tried to sit up and swing her legs round. She felt a bit dizzy and lay back awkwardly against the pillows. Michelle eventually came in and apologising to Pearl for being so late, said Jill would be in later but she would get her sorted out for today.

Pearl thought it strange that Jill hadn't come in, but perhaps she was ill that day. "What's happened, dear?" Pearl said. She could see Michelle's eyes were red rimmed and she looked as if she had been crying. "Are you all right?"

"Yes, Pearl, I'm fine. I'm afraid, though, I have some bad news," she said, her eyes brimming over again.

Pearl's heart started to thud in her chest as she knew then that one of the residents had passed away.

"Who is it?" she managed to gasp. "Not Hilda, is it? Or, no, not Arthur surely?" She knew it would be a sad day whoever it was.

"I'm so sorry, Pearl, it's Betty." Michelle just managed to catch Pearl as she almost toppled over.

"Oh, no. Oh dear Lord, not Betty. She was absolutely fine yesterday. She was showing me the crocheting she had almost finished." Pearl was distraught to think her close friend had passed away. That must have been what had upset poor old Ted, she thought, he was particularly fond of Betty. "I can't believe it. Do they know what it was?" she asked.

"She apparently had a massive heart attack sometime during the night, so she wouldn't have known anything about it. Janice went in as usual on her rounds when she was finishing her shift at five this morning and found her. She hadn't long gone, Janice said." She sat with Pearl for a moment to make sure she was all right. "The doctor was called, and the funeral home took her away an hour ago. Her family have been informed and they will be coming in the next day or two to pick up her things," Michelle explained. "I'm so sorry, Pearl, I know you and Betty got on so well."

Pearl felt such an overwhelming sense of sadness at the loss of her friend. They had spent many happy hours chatting about their families and Betty loved to knit for anyone who she knew was having a baby. They had laughed about Ted and his swearing and poor old Hilda with her troubles. Arthur had come under scrutiny as well, some of the things he came out with, although sad because he couldn't hear very well, had made them roar with laughter. Betty had chuckled when Pearl had told her about poor Susie and the cake on her birthday. Pearl was suddenly struck cold – how much worse is it going to be when it's Ruby? She had only known Betty for a few years, but the pain of losing her was still there. She had known Ruby since they were at school together. How on earth did she think it was going to be easy to say goodbye to her dearest and oldest friend?

'I'm not sure I'm up to going to Switzerland and seeing her go in front of me,' she worried. How awful was it going to be watching her children's pain and grief and having to deal with that as well as hers and that of her own children? 'I can't go and that's that!'

She would ring Susie and tell her about Betty and that they would have to manage without her. She was too old for all this and it wasn't fair!

She managed a cup of tea and decided to go back to her room after breakfast. The whole place was subdued, and she wasn't up to talking to anyone, not even old Ted who looked morose and was obviously heartbroken. She didn't feel able to console anyone and just wanted to be alone with her thoughts.

No one felt like meeting up for lunch, so they brought round sandwiches and hot drinks to those who wanted it in their rooms. After her sandwich, Pearl rang Susie. She had calmed down a little bit now and was feeling more objective, but still not sure she could manage the trip away.

"Oh, Mum, I'm so sorry. Look, I'm driving at the moment," Susie said on the hands-free phone, after her mother had tearfully told her about poor old Betty. "I'm only about ten minutes away, so I'll pop in and we can talk about it then, is that all right?"

"Oh, would you, darling? I'm all right, but I do need to speak to you about Switzerland, dear," Pearl said, relieved Susie was coming over.

Susie thought about what her mother had said about Switzerland and wondered if that meant she wasn't going to go. She wasn't sure how she felt about it. Part of her was relieved to think they wouldn't have to go and see all the pain and heartache, but on the other hand she wanted to be there for Ruby's family. She concentrated on her driving and thought she would see what her mum had to say.

Susie could see how devastated Pearl was at her friend's demise. She was looking sunken and frail sitting in her chair in her room; she hadn't put her radio on as she couldn't deal with the incessant chatter from the presenters today. She was just sitting there with her hands in her lap and staring into space with a faraway look on her face.

"Oh, Mum, how are you? I'm so sorry to hear about Betty." Susie hugged her mother, who looked relieved to see her daughter.

"Hello, darling, sorry to have called you in. I didn't know who else to talk to. Jill's busy with Betty's family and things." Pearl tailed off as the tears started to fall again.

"Mum, it's fine. I'll come whenever you need me. You were always there for me and Pete and now it's our turn to be here for you." Susie sat with her mother and gently stroking her hand said, "So have you changed your mind about going to Switzerland, then?"

"Oh, darling, I don't know!" Pearl wailed. "After Betty, er, you know, well, now Betty has gone and it was a shock and I'm so sad for her and her family, but it got me thinking, how can I just go and sit and watch Ruby die? I can't remember a time when I haven't known her, but with Betty it just happened, you see? With Ruby I'll, well, we all will know exactly what is going to happen and even worse, when! I'm not sure I'm up to that. Part of me thinks Ruby is being selfish for doing this and then the other part thinks *I'm* being selfish because I don't want it to happen, I'm so confused, darling."

Susie was lost for words. They had all been talking about how they were feeling and, yes, how hard it would be for Pearl to lose her friend, but Susie thought, Mum is ninety! She's the one having to face death every day and now watching one of her companions pass away has really brought it home to her just exactly what Ruby's death will mean to her.

"Mum, look," Susie said, "This has been a huge shock for you and it's too much for you to deal with at the moment. You're bound to be all over the place. What I suggest is that you don't do anything for now, we'll leave the trip planned as it is with the tickets and hotel etc. And then in a week or so, we'll see how you feel and if you still feel the same, we'll cancel everything. How does that sound?"

"Well, all right, dear, if you think that's best. I don't want anyone to lose money over this, but I just can't see me going." Pearl was still not sure what she should do, but perhaps Susie was right, and she should wait until the loss of Betty had eased.

"Do you think it might be an idea to speak to Ruby?" Susie asked hopefully. "Maybe speaking to her might make you feel better?"

"Yes, I might in a day or two, darling, not today. I think I might have a lie down if you don't mind, my head is pounding." Pearl just wanted to sleep and wake up with everything back to normal.

"I'll help you into bed and should I get one of the girls to bring you some painkillers? Or do you have any in here?" Susie stood up and shook out the duvet for Pearl.

"I have some in the top drawer if you could get me two and some water that will be lovely." Pearl sank back against the pillows after Susie had helped her in and gratefully sipped the water and waited for the tablets to soothe her headache. Susie kissed her cheek and promising to pop in the next day she left, she managed to catch Jill and asked her to pass on her condolences to Betty's family.

Pearl, Ted, Hilda and Arthur had all contributed to some flowers and Jill went to the funeral with Margaret as representatives for Willow Lodge.

It was a further two weeks before Pearl had summoned up the courage and the wherewithal to speak to Ruby again. She was acutely aware of the time passing so quickly, but just couldn't bring herself to talk to her. Tony had passed on the news to Ruby about Betty and, although she wanted to reach out and speak to Pearl, she knew it would be best to wait for Pearl to make the first move.

Chapter 26
July 2018

Pete had dropped in to sort out the Kindle for his mother and Jack was with Ruby; they made the connections and Pearl was able to see Ruby on the screen. Pearl wasn't sure how to start the conversation and she stared at Ruby for a long moment. Ruby was looking at her and suddenly she grinned, and Pearl could see again the young cheeky girl she was best friends with all those years ago.

"My dear, I'm so sorry I haven't spoken to you before now," Pearl said, once again fumbling with her tissue. It was true what they said, she thought, as you get older you revert back to being a baby – she seemed to cry at the drop of a hat these days! "They told you about dear old Betty?"

"Yes, sweetheart. Tony passed on the news and I'm so sorry for you all there. We lost John here a few days ago and it hits you hard, so don't worry about not being in touch," Ruby said. "It makes you all too aware how fragile life is, doesn't it?"

"Yes, I know we all have to go and I am resigned to the fact that it will be sooner rather than later, but it's still difficult, and with you, Ruby, well, your decision, I still can't work out whether it's best to go like Betty – just gone and that's it – or if your way is better." Pearl looked at Ruby and tried to see the answer in her face.

"The thing is, Pearl, I know exactly what you are thinking; you're thinking 'How can she be so selfish, going off and leaving all her family to suffer afterwards'…"

"Oh, no, dear, that's not it at all!" Pearl blustered.

"Come on, Pearl, don't you think I've thought the same thing? Every scenario you can come up with I've had the same, dear, but let me explain to you why I'm doing it," Ruby said gently. "I suppose, in a way, it could be seen as being selfish, but let me ask you a question. Is it selfish to want to spend however long I have left with my brain functioning normally so that I can say all the things I want to my boys and they to me, or is it better if I just quietly go doolally and they will have to see me knowing I don't know who they are or why they're there?"

"Well, when you put it like that, obviously you don't want that to happen," Pearl agreed.

"Or I could go at any time like your poor old Betty and never have the chance to say one more 'I love you' or even 'goodbye'. I know that could still happen at my age, but you see, Pearl, this way, the way I want it to happen is a choice – my choice and I'm in control." Ruby's voice was soft as she tried to get her friend to see it from her point of view. She knew it wasn't going to be easy; she'd had pretty much the same

192

conversations with Tony and Jack. "So, yes, it's selfish, but I'm actually doing it for my boys. Oh, they won't get it at first, but after some time has passed, they'll be grateful they didn't see me suffer or have to feel sorry for me. It's the only thing I have left to give them – and you," she added gently.

Pearl was crying softly on the other side of the screen and Ruby was sad she was upset, but she had no other way to explain it without it hurting a little bit.

"It's me that's being selfish, isn't it?" Pearl was snuffling and trying to check the tears. "All I'm thinking about it is what will I do without you."

"Well, that's the thing, you have your memories, sweetheart, and so you will remember me for the fun and good times we had, and so will the children. And don't forget, Pearl, at least this way you won't have to buy a hat because I certainly won't be getting married again!" Ruby was laughing now, and Pearl was half laughing, half crying.

"We did have some good times, and never fell out, did we?" Pearl said, remembering all the years they were together.

"Ah, yes all the parties; the holidays; watching the children grow up and get married then having their own children; and don't forget there were some bad times too. Remember that bloody swine Jim? What a horrid man he was to do that to both of us women who were in love with him!" Ruby said, still feeling the resentment after all these years.

"He was an unpleasant man most definitely. Edward wanted to punch him several times and, as you know, Edward didn't have a violent bone in his body, but something about Jim brought out the worst in him." Pearl was sorry now Edward hadn't punched him; it would have made them all feel better!

"Ha, ha, I would have liked to have seen that, but in the end, he wasn't worth the energy and I wouldn't have met Derek, so it all works out in the end, doesn't it?" Ruby laughed at the thought of dear Edward hitting anyone – at least she had remembered his name today, she thought thankfully.

"The other thing, Ruby," Pearl tried to get her words the way she wanted them, "I'm not really sure if I can go to Switzerland with you. I know I said I would, and I do want to be there for you, but I'm just not sure I can do it. I'm so sorry, it's just me being selfish again."

"Pearl, it's completely fine. I don't expect or demand anyone go with me, although I am pleased Tony and Jack will be there, but that's a decision only you can make. We can carry on talking on this marvellous system until I go, or you can just decide not to do it anymore. I think we both know how we feel about one another, don't we? Our love has always been there and seen us through, so, and only if you want, we don't actually have to say goodbye, it's entirely up to you." Ruby smiled at Pearl, drinking in her lovely face with her lipstick still in evidence even though she had lost most of it into her tissue. "Anyway, my dear, it's a lot to think about and I'm sure your girls will be round with the tea soon. I can hear the feet shuffling and the teacups rattling here so I'm going to get a cuppa and a biscuit, so I'll say goodbye, my dear, and remember how much I love you."

"I love you too, my dear, dear friend and thank you, Ruby, I'll speak to you soon." Pearl switched off the device and sat back in her chair. Well! she thought, whenever did Ruby become so wise and be the one to counsel Pearl, it always used to be the other way around!

One thing she was sure of though, whatever she decided about going to Switzerland, it was clear that Ruby was definitely going, and nothing was going to change her mind!

Chapter 27
October 1978

"I certainly wasn't expecting to be putting this coat on again so soon!" Pearl said to Edward as she took the dry-cleaning wrappers off her best black coat. She turned to Edward to see if he had taken the wrapper off the suit, she had had dry cleaned the day before and saw him wiping his eyes.

"Are you all right, love? Silly question, I know!" Pearl went over to where Edward stood and wrapped her arms around him.

Edward hugged her back as he cleared his throat. "Yes, I'm fine, I just wasn't expecting another funeral so soon and even though he wasn't my real dad I grew to love old Ken in a way, and he was the best thing to happen to Mum, God bless her!"

"I honestly don't think he felt he could carry on without her; you often hear of people dying of a broken heart and I think that's exactly what happened to Ken," Pearl said. "We have time for a cuppa if you want one, love, or maybe something a bit stronger?"

"Now, that's a good idea! I might just have a small brandy – just for medicinal purposes, obviously!" he said, smiling at Pearl.

It had certainly been a year for funerals, thought Pearl as she poured the drinks. First Ruby had lost her father Alf in the January; he was in his early seventies and hadn't been well for a long while, but it was still a shock when he had a stroke followed by a heart attack and was gone a week later. Pearl's beloved father John had gone early summer; at seventy-five he seemed to be fit and active and then one day he fell over at home. Gwen called the doctor out and he had had a brain haemorrhage – he never recovered, and they buried him two weeks later.

At the end of August, Eleanor had suffered from a bad chest infection, she was hospitalised and diagnosed with pneumonia – she had spent some time in hospital but the fluid on her lungs finally drowned her and now just six weeks later Ken had passed away in his sleep.

He was ninety and so it was classed as old age, but Pearl still believed he was broken hearted after losing Eleanor.

"Susie and Dan will be there along with Pete – I think he's coming on his own." Pearl wasn't sure who Pete was seeing half the time. She only knew he was with someone when they turned up – most of the time unannounced – for a meal or a cuppa! "I think they will only stay for a little while though as Dan's mother is at home with the little ones. Josh is only a few weeks old so it's a bit much for her, although at seven and four Caroline and Fleur will help her as they love their little brother."

"Are Ruby and her lot coming?" Edward asked, feeling much better after the brandy and now straightening his tie.

"Yes, they are meeting us at the church. Tony and Jeannie will be there, and I think Jack and Maria are coming. Derek said he'll try and save a parking spot if we're not too far behind them." Pearl was ready. She applied a last slick of lipstick and waited for Edward to put his jacket on.

"Right! Let's go! I won't need the order of service; I know all the bloody words to *Abide with Me* now!" Edward said wryly.

They did indeed sing 'Abide with Me' and after the service and burial they all gathered in the local pub for Ken's wake. His two children were there, and they were pleased to see Edward. They had only met a few times, but they were very pleasant. His son especially reminded Edward of Ken; he now said to Edward, "I believe Dad has left you something in his will."

"Oh, no," Edward blustered, "I certainly don't want anything, whatever your dad left belongs to you."

"Well, he has left you five hundred pounds and we really do hope you will accept it. He was very fond of you and your family," his son Richard said, smiling at Pearl and Edward.

"Well, that's very generous, but he was your dad not mine, although I was fond of him and he was like a father to me at times." Edward was astounded at the amount Ken had left him, the dear old soul.

Richard said he would be receiving a letter from his solicitor and it would make the old boy very happy if Edward would accept the bequest.

The cheque duly arrived and was deposited in the bank. It sat there for a few weeks and Edward had been thinking what to do with the windfall and suddenly it came to him. A holiday! Ken and his mother had loved travelling and spent a fair bit of their time together seeing the sights in Europe. Maybe, just maybe he and Pearl could have a week away and see if Derek and Ruby could go too?

It would be like a homage to Ken to use the money for a spot of travelling, he thought.

It was all arranged for June the following year! Derek and Ruby had been only too keen to go with them and soon Pearl and Ruby were shopping for their holiday essentials.

They had decided to go to Greece this time and the girls were busy planning what they wanted to see as it was full of culture. Derek wanted to know if the nearest bar was in walking distance from their hotel! Edward was just pleased they had been able to organise it and he silently thanked Ken and hoped he would approve.

Chapter 28
June 1979

The plane took off and Pearl visibly relaxed; she wasn't sure she would ever get used to this flying lark, but it was exciting at the same time. It was nice not to have any children with them; it meant they could relax and stay out later in the evenings if they wanted to.

Pearl thought though, it would be nice to go with Susie's children and see them enjoying the sunshine and the golden beaches; much nicer than dear old Great Yarmouth! She would speak to Susie when they got back and see what they thought – maybe they could go the following year. We haven't even got there yet and I'm already thinking about when I get back, she chided herself.

A few hours later and, with all the unpacking done, they were sitting in a taverna having a meal and a few drinks. "Now, Edward, go easy on the funny food and the booze mate, you don't want a dodgy belly like last time!" Derek laughed.

"Ha, ha! Very funny!" Edward laughed along with the girls. "I'm only having a couple tonight – pacing myself, you see, and you can't go wrong with steak, can you?" On cue the waiter brought out their food. They had all ordered steaks and a Greek salad to share. Pearl and Ruby were drinking gin and tonic and the men were having bottled beer – just to be on the safe side! They spent a pleasant evening chatting and laughing; all four relaxed and having a good time. They made their way back to the hotel and arranged what time they would meet up for breakfast.

"Are you tired, darling?" Edward said to Pearl once they in their room. "Do you fancy a last nightcap on the balcony? It's a lovely evening and still feels warm – not like back home!"

"Yes, that sounds like a good idea, but I might just have a cuppa instead, but you have one if you like," Pearl said, busying herself with the tiny travel kettle and the plastic cups they had brought with them. Edward opened his bottle of duty-free brandy and poured some into the plastic cup Pearl handed to him. They sat on the balcony listening to the crickets and the soft swoosh as the waves hit the beach below them.

Edward raised his cup to the sky and said, "Here's to you, Ken, what a wonderful person you were, and it was a pleasure to have known you."

"Cheers," said Pearl toasting with her tea. "Isn't this lovely? I'm feeling all the stresses of the past few months just falling away. I think this is exactly what we all needed, darling." She reached across and kissed Edward warmly.

"Yes, I know what you mean; it's the perfect tonic for us. Right then, darling, have you finished your tea?

Let's get into bed. It's strange only having a sheet to cover us when we are so used to blankets!"

The following morning, they all met up for breakfast and sat in the sunshine planning their day. There was an archaeological site a bus ride away with the most stunning mosaics the guide Ruby was reading stated. They waited for the bus just outside their hotel and soon arrived at the site; they spent a lovely day wandering around the ruins, marvelling at the mosaics and soaking up the culture.

The week passed with them relaxing by the pool and swimming in the beautiful Aegean Sea.

On the day before they were due to fly home, the girls went off to shop for trinkets and souvenirs to take home and Edward and Derek decided to go off on their own and try to find a gift each for Ruby and Pearl. They found just what they were looking for in a little jewellers in a back street and later that evening as they were having their last meal, they presented the girls with delicate gold necklaces. Pearl's had a tiny pearl set into the pendant and Ruby had a tiny ruby in hers. They were delighted and Pearl could see the loving look Ruby gave to Derek and was so pleased for her friend. As he had got older Derek was even more handsome, Pearl thought, his salt and pepper hair suited him and with his suntan she thought he looked a bit like Omar Sharif, the gorgeous Egyptian actor. She only had eyes for her darling Edward though.

"I'd like to propose a toast," Derek announced. "Here's to you Edward and Pearl for asking us along and being such bloody good friends! Cheers!"

"Well, now, if we're toasting, I'd like to propose a toast to Ken and all the other poor souls we have lost this past year. Cheers!" Edward said and they all raised their glasses again.

"I would like to toast my wonderful friend Pearl, without whom none of us would be here," declared Ruby. "Friends to the end!" She chinked her glass with Pearl.

"My toast is to all of us; to love and laughter!" Pearl said.

They all toasted one another and declared the holiday had been a success. Although they were reluctant for it to end, they were all looking forward to getting home and having a proper cup of tea!

Chapter 29
July 2018

"Hello, Mum," Tony said as he bent to kiss his mother's cheek. "This came for you. It looks official so I brought it straightaway." He handed her the large envelope in his hand.

"Ah, yes, I expect it's the final approval with the letter from Dr Sampson giving me the okay to go ahead; they said it would arrive about four weeks before I go." Ruby opened the envelope and it was indeed the approval she had been waiting for. "I just need to sign it and get it back to them as soon as possible; can you wait while I read through it and then send it back for me?"

"Of course, Mum. I'll go and rustle up some tea while you have a read, or I could check it with you, if you like?" Tony couldn't believe they were talking about this as if they were discussing an insurance policy or something instead of an end of life approval!

"Yes, okay, darling, thank you. I'll have a read through and if I get stuck you can help me out when you get back." Ruby saw her name and the date of the 'procedure' on the first page and a frisson of nerves mixed with relief came over her. Of course, she was nervous; it wasn't something she'd ever done before, was it? At eighty-nine she had been hoping for just a quiet decline; sleeping and not doing much at all after all the years of hard work she had done, but it wasn't to be, and she was still resolute in her decision that this way was definitely the best outcome for her and everyone else.

Tony returned with a tea tray and watched his mum reading. In his mind he took picture after picture of her and tried to imprint them onto his memory. His heart was breaking that in a little under four weeks she would be gone from his life forever. He shook himself and made his way over to her with a smile plastered to his face.

"Here we are, and as usual a plate of biscuits – they must have shares in McVities, they never seem to run out, do they?" he prattled on as he poured the tea.

"Mmm? Sorry, love, I was just reading this bit about afterwards, you know, what you want to do with me, when, well afterwards. I need to confirm it will be a cremation and then they will contact you within a week or so to fly back and collect the ashes, is that all right, dear?" Ruby looked up to see the tears coursing down Tony's face and his whole body was heaving with sobs. "Oh, my darling, I'm so sorry, how insensitive of me. It's just reading through this, it's as if it's happening to someone else; it all becomes slightly impersonal."

Ruby was distraught to see her beloved son so upset. She gently pushed over a box of tissues and waited for him to collect himself. She so wanted to hug him and cuddle him like she used to do when he fell off his bike or scraped his knees playing football, but she was afraid he might reject her – after all, it was her fault he was upset, not a game or a bike.

"It's me that should say sorry, Mum. I know you need us to be strong and support you and I do, I really do, I just can't seem to hold back these bloody tears. It's like a dam building up then all of a sudden it bursts and off I go!" Tony blew his nose hard and smiled at his mum with watery eyes. "I'm okay now, and yes, me and Jack will fly back the following week and pick you, err, them up. We will book the service and have a scattering ceremony for you. Are you still sure you want to be scattered in the sea? Oh, and have you sorted out which music you want playing?" He could feel the tears threatening again and his throat became painful, but he forced it back. "You can choose up to three I think it is."

"Oh, my dear, I completely forgot to tell you, I was thinking of some songs the other week and that set me off!" She went on to tell him about the least appropriate songs she had thought of and they both roared with laughter.

"I need another bloody tissue now!" Tony said wiping his eyes; it was like an emotional rollercoaster, he thought. "So, do you want *Always look on the bright side* at the beginning or the end?" They were off again, and this time Ruby reached for the tissues.

"Well, I have given it some serious thought and I would really like some Glenn Miller – not *A String of*

Pearls though, that's Pearl and Edward's song obviously, but any of the others and maybe a classical piece? You know I'm having Vivaldi at the clinic?" Ruby hoped she wasn't being too ridiculous in her choices, but she really didn't want any hymns to be played – they reminded her too much of all funerals she had already been to!

"Okay. Well you always used to like Bach, what was the piece you liked? *Air*, wasn't it? Or, I know, what about Pachelbel's *Canon*? They are both lovely; which one, Mum, or both?" Tony was trying to hum *Canon* under his breath. It was sad and it would remind him off his mother, but it was soothing at the same time.

"Oh, yes, either of those is perfect. I think I prefer *Canon* though, if that's all right? It's not too sad though, is it?" Ruby couldn't bear the thought of everyone weeping and wailing.

"No, it's lovely and it will be perfect. Right then, I've jotted them down and I'll let Jack know what you have chosen, and we'll get it organised. Now have you signed all the relevant bits?" Tony gestured to the paperwork Ruby still held in her hand.

"Yes, darling, it's all done. Would you put it in the envelope for me, please? My hands get a bit shaky and my fingers don't seem to want to work today." Ruby hated the way her hands were; all gnarled up now with lumps and bits appearing everywhere – blasted thing, she thought, cursing the arthritis that was seizing up her joints.

They finished their tea and sat close to one another, each of them silently soaking one another into their hearts, until eventually Tony had to leave. "I'll pop back in a day or two then, Mum?" he said with a heavy heart sad to be leaving. "Are you talking to Pearl again soon? Do you need help with the Kindle or are you okay with it now?" he asked.

"I think we will be in touch again soon, although I'm not sure when, but I think we will be okay, thank you, darling. It's just the timing we have to get right, but Jill over there will let me know, I expect." Ruby held onto her son as he hugged her, and she could feel her emotions start to take over. "Bye, my darling, and thank you, I love you!"

"I love you too, Mum, take care and I'll see you soon." Tony took one long last lingering look at his mum before he left.

As he was driving home his thoughts were taken back to the day, they had lost Dad.

Chapter 30
December 1988

"Mr Clancy? Sorry to bother you but there is a call for you on line two." The young secretary had only been with the company for a few weeks and was a bit in awe of her new boss; she wasn't happy about interrupting his meeting, but it sounded urgent.

"I'm in a meeting, can you take a message and I'll call them back please, Julie?" Tony was head of the finance department. It was an important quarterly meeting to discuss the forthcoming budgets and he was keen to get it finished today.

"Err, I'm really sorry, sir, but it sounded urgent," Julie said awkwardly.

With a sigh Tony apologised to the others seated around the boardroom table and strode quickly back to his office.

"Hello? Hello? Who is this?" he barked into the phone. He heard sobbing and then a familiar voice came through. "Mum? Is that you? What's the matter? Are you all right? I can't hear you very well."

The voice on the other end came through muffled and he was struggling to hear what his mum was saying.

"It's Dad, darling, can you come home now, please?" Ruby was beside herself with grief. "I've taken him a cup of tea and he's gone, darling."

"Gone? Gone where? For a walk?" Tony couldn't understand what the matter was.

"No, dear, he's still here, but he's gone, I've called the doctor and he's on his way, but he's cold!" Ruby was crying hysterically now, and Tony suddenly realised what she meant.

"Oh, no. Oh god. I'm on my way, Mum. Have you rung Jack? Don't worry, I'll ring him, and we'll be there as soon as we can." Tony put the phone down and shouted to Julie as he left, "I've got an emergency at home, Julie, can you tell the others in there?" He gestured to the boardroom. "Tell them I'll reschedule as soon as I can, but I'm likely not going to be in for the rest of the week, take any messages and pass them to Brian – thanks." Picking up the phone again he called Jack. "Bruv? It's me. Bruv, can you get home to Mum and Dad's as soon as? You'll get there before me I reckon. I'm so sorry, bruv, but it looks as if Dad has passed away. Mum's beside herself and the docs on his way. I'll be as quick as I can!" and he flew off out the building to get to his parents' house.

Jack had hardly managed to say anything other than 'hello', but he jumped up and, pulling on his jacket, told his team he'd ring them later, but he had to dash off urgently.

Ruby and Derek lived just outside Norwich in Costessey, about five miles from the city. They had bought the house when they had been married for a few years and they loved it there; it was quieter than living in the city but close enough to still get in for shopping etc.

Jack arrived and jumped out of the car as soon as he had switched off the engine; he saw the doctor's car parked in the drive.

"Mum? Mum? Where are you?" he called frantically.

"I'm in here, dear," Ruby replied from the kitchen. "The doctor is with Dad now."

"Oh, Mum!" Jack was aghast at his mother's face; her eyes were red from crying and her skin had a ghostly grey pallor, he took her in his arms, and she started sobbing. "What happened, Mum?"

"Dad was saying he had indigestion this morning, so I nipped to the shop for some of those tablets – Rennies or something. Anyway, I thought I'd get a few groceries while I was out. When I came back, I put the shopping away and put the kettle on to make us a cup of tea and when I went into the living room he was, he was, just sitting there. I thought he must have nodded off and he didn't answer when I called him and then I touched him, and he was cold. Oh, darling, he must have gone while I was at the shop and he was all alone!" Ruby was tearing her tissue to bits and wringing her hands.

"Mum?" Tony shouted from the front door.

"In the kitchen, bruv," Jack called back, and Tony came straight in.

"What's the doc said?" Tony asked, taking over from Jack with his mum so Jack could put the kettle on.

"He hasn't been here long, so he might be out in a little while," Ruby said, glad to see her boys but devastated about Derek. She felt terribly guilty for not being here when he needed her most.

Tony looked at his mum and said, "Sit tight in here with Jack and I'll ring Pearl. I can go and get her, she'll be over in a flash, Mum, and she'll sort you out."

"Okay, dear. Yes, Pearl will be just the right person. Can you call her, Tony?" Ruby knew her friend would be the best comfort she could have today.

"Ooh, there's the blasted phone. You go on through, love, and put the kettle on and I'll see if I can answer it in time." Pearl hurried up the path and managed to get to the phone in time. She dropped her shopping bags on the hall chair while Susie made her way into the kitchen. "Hello? Oh, hello, Tony, or is it Jack? I can never tell you two apart on the phone. You've only just caught me; I was out doing some Christmas shoppi... WHAT! Oh, my god! No, no, dear, it's fine, you stay there with your mum. Susie is with me and she will run me over to you, I'm sure. Yes, dear, I'm on my way – oh, I'll get Edward too. Is the doctor still there? Just gone? Okay, yes, my dear, don't worry, I'll be there in a jiffy. SUS... oh, there you are." Pearl was just about to tell Susie not to bother with the kettle, when Susie had heard the word doctor and came in to see what was going on.

"What's happened, Mum?" Susie looked anxiously at her mum, "Is Ruby all right?"

"Oh, my dear, Uncle Derek has passed away. Tony and Jack are with Ruby now and the doctor has just left – would you run me over there?" Pearl stuffed the shopping in the hall cupboard and buttoned her coat back up.

"Yes, of course, Mum. Do you want to ring Dad and we can pick him up on the way?" Susie knew her dad would want to be there; he was very fond of Derek and it would break his heart.

"Yes, I'll see if I can get hold of him." Pearl dialled the station and was put through. She explained to Edward what had happened, and he said he would be ready and waiting.

The ambulance was there when they arrived, and they were loading Derek into the back. Susie parked outside on the roadway so they could have easy access to leave, but obviously there was no urgency – not now.

Pearl went into the house and heard voices from the kitchen; she went in followed by Edward. Ruby sat at the table clutching a tissue in one hand and their wedding photograph in the other. "Oh, my darling." Pearl rushed over and enveloped Ruby in her arms. "I am so, so, sorry."

Jack busied himself with the kettle again as Edward came over and shook his hand then hugged him. He did the same with Tony and said how sorry he was.

Ruby was telling Pearl what she had told Jack and Tony when they arrived about finding Derek in the chair. Susie went into the hallway to ring Dan and explain she would be late back.

"The doc said it was a heart attack. The post-mortem should confirm it, he said, but he was pretty certain by looking at Dad," Tony explained.

"He was only sixty-six, that's no age nowadays," Jack said. "And he was reasonably fit, kept himself active, and tried to eat the right foods."

"I know, lad, I know." Edward was shaking his head; he couldn't believe Derek had gone. They had been close all these years and the two couples did everything together. He said to Jack, "There's just no way of knowing, I suppose. When your time's up, it's up."

Pearl and Ruby were sitting together with Susie and Pearl was thinking however will Ruby cope without him? Despite being a strong woman, Ruby depended on Derek for almost everything.

Ruby was thinking the same and said the same to the others, "Oh, Pearl, however will I manage? We were only talking last night about what we're going to do now he's finally retired. He was looking forward to putting his feet up. He was on about getting a dog to go for walks." Ruby dissolved into floods of tears again as she thought of all the things they were looking forward to and now all of it gone in an instant. "I never got to say goodbye or tell him I loved him," she wailed.

"Derek knew how much you loved him, darling, as we all did," Pearl said soothingly.

Tony and Jack were discussing which funeral directors they were using and talking about the practicalities of organising everything with Edward. Edward offered to help with anything they needed – financially or otherwise.

"Dad had all kinds of insurance policies, so once we've sorted that out Mum should be okay, but thank you, Edward," Tony said. He was still in shock and the thought of getting everything sorted out was more than he could cope with at the moment.

They sat with Ruby for a while longer and Pearl offered to stay the night with her, unless she wanted to come with them back to their house. Ruby decided she wanted to be in her own bed and so Susie took Edward home and he had a meal with her and Dan.

Tony and Jack had called their wives and they were coming over tomorrow as Ruby couldn't face anyone else tonight; her head was aching, and her heart was broken. The doctor had left her a sedative and Pearl watched her swallow the pills and settled her down for the night.

"I'll be in the spare room, darling. Call me if you need anything, won't you?" Pearl said as she left her friend to sleep.

The post-mortem confirmed the doctor's diagnosis; Derek had died of a massive heart attack.

The funeral was held ten days later and there was a huge turnout from the factory he had worked in for over forty years. The service was lovely and there wasn't a dry eye in the house. Ruby retired early from work and spent most of her days rattling around in the big house alone. Pearl went to see her as much as she could and, of course, her sons and their wives were constant visitors, but Ruby couldn't seem to get over losing Derek. Her guilt at not being with him when he died was consuming her; the doctor had put her on anti-depressants to try and help her get her life back on track.

It was a chance meeting six years later that helped her find love again.

Chapter 31
July 1994

"I'm not sure I can make it tonight, Pearl. I'm really sorry, but I'm not sure I'm up to going out." Ruby had phoned Pearl to cry off from the evening out they had planned.

"Well, it's up to you, sweetheart. It's only a few of us going down the pub for our wedding anniversary – we're going to have a big do in two years' time when it's our fiftieth, but it would do you good to get out," Pearl said. She understood Ruby's reluctance to go out, but she was becoming a recluse and it wasn't doing her any good mentally being shut away every day – it was so unlike the Ruby Pearl knew. She was at a loss how to help her old friend.

"Tell you what, we are going at seven thirty p.m. so if you change your mind, let me know and Edward will nip over and get you about seven. How does that sound?"

"Yes, okay, well, I'll see how I feel later, and I'll let you know," Ruby replied.

Pearl was ironing Edward's shirt later that afternoon when the phone rang. Her hair was in curlers and she had a face pack on. She hoped whoever it was wasn't trying to sell her anything, the face pack was drying, and it was painful to move her lips too much!

"Hello?" Pearl said into the mouthpiece, careful not to get any of the goo on it.

"It's me," Ruby said. "Are you all right? You sound as if your face is swollen!?"

"Oh, hello, dear. No, it's one of those face pack things. Susie told me about them, so I thought I'd have a go for tonight – anything to ward off the advancing years! Ha! Ha!" Pearl could feel the pack cracking across her cheeks as she started to laugh. "I'll have to go and wash it off in a minute. I was trying to get Edward's shirt ready while I waited. Anyway, how are you?" she said hopefully.

"When you said there was just a few of you going, how many exactly?" Ruby asked.

Yes! Pearl thought, she is going to come out! She said casually, "Well, there's me and Edward, of course. Susie, Dan and Pete and some of their lot will be there. I think your Tony and Jeannie might pop in. Obviously, Jack and Maria are away on holiday so they won't be coming and a few of Edward's workmates said they would be there. It's just a few drinks and some nibbles, we're not having a proper meal."

"What are you wearing?" Ruby asked next.

"I picked up a lovely cornflower blue summer dress last week – Edward says it brings out the colour of my eyes, and my navy jacket in case it gets cooler later on," Pearl said. Then realising what she had said, she was horrified she had mentioned about Edward and her eyes – it was always something Derek had said to Ruby.

"Oh, that sounds lovely and yes, the blue always looks good on you. I think I might come if you don't mind and I was going to wear a dark pink skirt and a white top. Will that be okay?" Ruby asked.

"Oh, darling, that will be perfect. Look, Edward will come and pick you up at seven and bring your things in case you want to stay over. We can have a natter tomorrow then and Edward can run you back after lunch." Pearl was so pleased Ruby was coming but hoped she hadn't put too much pressure on her.

"I think it will do me good to get out, you know, you are right. I'll bring my stuff but if I decide to go home, I can get a taxi." Ruby had thought she couldn't face another night in, and she wasn't getting any better sitting around expecting Derek to walk in.

It was a lively evening, and everyone was enjoying themselves. Ruby was so glad she hadn't stayed in; this was just what she needed. She had decided to stay at Pearl's tonight, and she felt better knowing she wouldn't be alone.

One of Edward's work mates had bought her a drink and she sat chatting to him in the garden of the pub. He was telling her he hadn't been out hardly at all since his wife had died a few months ago and Ruby could see how much he still loved her. She told him about Derek, and they found they had a lot in common.

His name was Colin Hughes and as the evening drew to a close, he plucked up the courage to ask if she wanted to go to dinner with him the following week. To her surprise she said yes, they had a wonderful time and so began their courtship.

Pearl and Edward were pleased to see Ruby looking animated again and often teased Ruby about their match making skills. Edward knew Colin was a decent bloke and would be good for Ruby.

A year later, Colin asked her to marry him and a year after that they married. Pearl and Edward were witnesses – once again – and Ruby became Mrs Hughes. She still loved Derek, but this was more like companionship and she grew to love Colin in a different way.

They had ten happy years together until Colin succumbed to cancer and passed away in 2006.

Chapter 32
August 2018

Susie and Dan were sitting on the patio of their home indulging in a late afternoon glass of wine, enjoying the sunshine; now the searing heat of the day was cooling down it was too nice to sit indoors.

"Has your mum said anymore about what she plans to do about Switzerland?" Dan asked.

"When I saw her yesterday, she said she was still confused and not sure what she wants to do. I think she feels she needs to be there for Ruby but on the other hand just doesn't think she can bear it!" Susie replied, feeling pretty much the same herself.

"Yes, it's a bloody difficult decision to make, isn't it? I was thinking though, darling, either I could stay here and be with Pearl at the, err, on the day, so she isn't on her own when the time comes and you and Pete can go with the others, or, if we could persuade her to come along but not decide if she wants to be at the clinic, I could again sit with her at the hotel or take her out somewhere. The hire car will be there anyway. What do you think?" Dan had thought it through and, although he wanted to support Susie at the clinic, he knew Pete would be there and she would be all right.

"Oh, darling, yes, that's a good idea. I'll give Pete a ring and see what he thinks, but if we could persuade Mum to go it would be better. I'll see if he's in now." Susie got up and went into the kitchen where her mobile phone was sitting on the side.

Pete thought either idea was sound, but he, too, was keen on trying to persuade Pearl to go, just in case she did change her mind and want to be with Ruby.

"We can always say the fresh mountain air would do her good; and it would to be honest, I know the home is fantastic for Mum, but it wouldn't hurt her to get out for a few days," Pete said to his sister. "Do you want me to pop over and see her or are you going?"

"Let's both go tomorrow, if you've nothing planned?" Susie said. "It might be better if we are both there."

"Yep, okay, I'm free all day, so, what? Usual time about eleven ish?" Pete said. "I'll pick up some flowers for her too; cheer her up a bit!"

Pearl was sitting waiting for Susie and Pete to arrive. She had an idea they were going to try and persuade her to go, and she really wanted to, she really did. How could she let her best friend down when she needed her at this time more than any other time throughout their lives? But Pearl just couldn't see past seeing Ruby lying in that bed cheerfully swallowing down God knows what and giving everyone a merry little wave and then dying!

If it was breaking her heart just to think of it now, how much worse will it be when they are all there watching and waiting?

She was so confused and a part of her had wished Ruby had never said anything and just got on with it! And how would Ruby feel if the tables were turned and it was you? She chided herself. Oh, dear, it was making her headache just going back and forth, and she was in a complete quandary.

Pete handed the flowers to his mum and bent to kiss her. "Hello, Mum, you look well," he said, although in truth, Pearl was looking more and more frail each time he saw her.

"Thank you, darling, these are lovely." She inhaled the gorgeous scent of the carnations and freesias in the bouquet. "I'm all right, love. It's lovely and warm this year, we are usually having thunderstorms and whatnot by now, but there's not a cloud in the sky and hasn't been for the last few days," Pearl prattled on.

Susie also kissed her mother, and then went in search of Michelle to see if there was a vase, she could put the flowers in. After chatting with Michelle and arranging the flowers she carried back the tea and sat with Pete and her mum.

"So, have you been talking anymore to Ruby?" Pete was asking Pearl.

"Oh, yes, dear, we are getting to be quite good with it now. We arrange a time after we have finished so that we know when one or the other will call next; it's working out beautifully." Pearl was enjoying her chats with Ruby. They didn't say much more about the looming date and they spent the time reminiscing about their lives instead. In a way it had brought them even closer, if such a thing were possible. Pearl was especially glad as there had been the nearly eight-year period when they hadn't been in touch very much.

"How is Ruby?" Susie asked, joining in the conversation and handing her mother a cup of tea. Pearl's hand shook slightly as she took it, and it rattled in the saucer before she was able to right it.

"She is very well. Well no, she's not, but you know Ruby, she is just the same, hiding her pain and her real feelings," Pearl said, thinking that every time she spoke to Ruby, her face was a little more pinched with the pain she was coping with.

"Yes," said Susie, "Jeannie was telling me her joints have swollen up in the heat and they have extra fans in her room to try and keep her cool." Jeannie had also said that Ruby had wished she'd booked the clinic earlier so that it was all over – but she didn't think her mother would take that very well, so Susie said no more.

"Ah, poor old Ruby," Pearl sighed, "its horrid getting older you know, darlings – or as Ted would say it's a bugger!"

They chatted about various ailments they all had as a result of growing old; Dan's knees, Pete's eyes and Susie's back and discussed all the different tablets one could take to alleviate the pain until you rattled!

Pete then said to his mum, "Mum, we need to talk about Switzerland."

"I know, dear, I still can't make up my mind though!" Pearl said, the anguish visible in her eyes.

"Well, Dan has come up with an idea – well, two ideas really, but we think the second one is probably the best for you." Susie outlined the two options.

"So, you're saying I should go and then decide how I feel on the day? I don't have to decide now?" Pearl was relieved she could leave it for now.

"Yes, exactly!" said Pete. "Dan has said if you really can't face it at the, erm, well, at the last minute, then you don't have to, and let's face it, none of us do really, but he will stay with you or drive you off somewhere and it will do you good to get away for a few days anyway. And you can have your last day with Ruby before she goes in, but you will be there if you change your mind and decide you do want to. Does that make sense?" Pete was jumbling up the words in his awkwardness.

"Oh, yes, dear, perfect sense. Oh, that's made me feel so much better. Thank you and please give Dan my thanks too, he is so good to do this for me." The colour had come back to Pearl's face and she was instantly livelier than when they first arrived.

"Excellent!" Susie said. "Right, that's all settled then. I was dreading the thought of leaving you here to worry about everything and with no one to talk to, Mum."

"We'll let Tony know, shall we? Or are you talking to Ruby soon?" Pete was glad to see his mother looking a bit more animated.

"We've arranged to have a natter tomorrow afternoon, but you can tell him if you want to before then." For the first time in weeks, Pearl was actually looking forward to speaking with Ruby.

The following day Pearl connected the Kindle to Ruby and was happy to see her smiling face. Ruby didn't look as drawn as she had the last time they had spoken.

"Hello, my dear," Ruby said, "I thought Milly was coming over today?"

"Yes, darling, she will be here in about half an hour. You can see the baby then; she has grown and is utterly adorable. Has Megan had any news yet?" Pearl was excited to see the baby and show off her latest great-great-granddaughter.

"I think they are taking her in tomorrow to induce her if nothing happens tonight." Ruby replied. "I am keeping my fingers crossed for her!"

"I'm sure she will be all right and someone will let me know as soon as she has had it. Now, sweetheart, before Milly gets here, I wanted to let you know I am coming to Switzerland after all! I've been a silly old fool, I know, but, well, anyway I'm now going. I still haven't made a decision about the clinic yet, but at least I will be there close by and Dan will stay with me if needs be." Pearl saw her old friend's eyes light up.

"Ah, Pearl, that is wonderful. I never intended to put any pressure on you or anyone, but it will be marvellous just to know you will be there, and don't worry about the clinic, I understand completely." Ruby was overjoyed Pearl was going. It would be a little bit like all their other fabulous trips, albeit this one will have a different ending.

Pearl looked around and saw Milly making her way over with the car seat.

"Perfect timing!" she said to Ruby. "Here's Milly and darling Olivia! Look Milly, can you see Ruby? Isn't it wonderful? I don't think I'll ever get over it!" She cooed over Olivia as Milly took the sleeping baby out of her car seat and gently placed her in Pearl's arms.

"Oh, my, she's a beauty, Milly. How is Harry with her?" Ruby asked, peering into the screen to see her.

"Hi, Ruby, he's actually really good. To be honest, we weren't sure if he would be jealous, but now he knows she's not going to steal any of his cars or his favourite teddy Menot, he is happy for her to be there." Milly smiled at Ruby.

"What on earth sort of teddy is a Menot?" Pearl and Ruby asked – both at the same time!

"Ha! Ha! When he was born, he was given a teddy elephant. It was called Forget-me-not, but he never could say it as it was a mouthful, so he used to say the last part – Me-not – so now it's a Menot!" Milly explained.

"Ah, that's wonderful, Milly. You have such a lovely little family," Ruby said, thinking back to the days when her babies were small.

"Any news with Megan yet?" Milly asked. "Mum said she was now two weeks overdue?"

Ruby brought her up to date with the news and promised to let everyone know as soon as she did.

"Thanks, Ruby. I hope you both have a wonderful in Switzerland, Gran told us you were going. It's somewhere I've always fancied, but a bit too expensive and with the children now. I think Spain or Portugal might be our holiday destination for the next few years, although with the weather here even Great Yarmouth is nice!" Milly laughed. "Well, I only popped in to show off this little one, so I'd better get on. She'll need a feed soon and I have to pick Harry up from Scott's mums. He had a sleepover yesterday, so I'm sure she's had enough by now! Give my love to everyone and I'll see you soon! Love you – byeeee."

"Goodbye, my dear, take care and love you too," Ruby called out.

Milly kissed Pearl and promised to come again soon.

"Sorry, dear," said Pearl unsure of what exactly she was apologising for, but feeling she needed to.

"Not at all, Pearl, that's exactly how it should be. You see, we both got to say goodbye and that we loved each other!" Ruby said, her eyes shining.

228

Megan's baby was born the following afternoon; it was a little girl and they named her Alice Ruby. Ruby was thrilled when she was given the news. She wasn't normally given to fanciful notions, but she felt that now her replacement had arrived she could go in peace. Out with the old and in with the new, her dear old mum used to say!

Photographs were duly taken and sent round to everyone via their phones and Tony and Jeannie had sent some to Pearl's family so she could see the new addition to the Clancy family.

Chapter 33
March 2000

Pearl didn't think the millennium was getting off to a good start! Her mum Gwen had passed away at the end of last year; at ninety-five, she had lived a full life and passed away peacefully in her sleep. Pearl missed her every day and three months later she still found herself almost on the point of ringing her mum to ask her something or to give her some family news when she had to stop herself short and she remembered again that her mum was no longer there!

Now Edward was ill; he had suffered from a heavy cold over the winter and a chest infection had seen him confined to bed for two weeks. Pearl was concerned about him as he was losing weight and seemed to be constantly having bouts of sickness and diarrhoea. She had begged him to go to the doctors and, not one to bother about it, eventually even he realised there was something wrong and he needed to go and get checked out.

He came back from his appointment and told Pearl he had to go back the next day with some samples to be tested.

"Oh, dear, I hope it's nothing to worry about, but it's good the doctor is doing something," Pearl said. She had made some soup as he couldn't seem to keep much else down at the moment.

"Yes, I'll be fine, darling, don't worry about me. The doc has given some tablets to take in the meantime. It will get sorted soon and I'll be as right as rain, you'll see!" He bravely ate half a bowl of soup but was up in the night being sick again.

The results came back, and Edward was told he had bowel cancer. Unfortunately, the specialist told him he had been suffering from it for several months and all they would offer now was palliative care. He was in hospital for two weeks with an intravenous drip to try and re-hydrate him.

Susie and Dan visited every day, taking Pearl so she could sit with him. Pete was there too, and it was obvious to them all that Edward wasn't coming home.

Ruby and Colin came too and Tony, Jack and their families all visited over the following days.

They all tried to keep his spirits up and took him in little treats to tempt his appetite. He couldn't eat fruit, so they took him biscuits and little cakes the younger children had made for him.

"I'm not long for this world now, darling," he said hoarsely to Pearl one evening when she was visiting – Susie had left them alone for a few minutes privacy as it was clear her dad wanted to speak to her mum alone.

"Oh, my darling, please don't say that, the doctors can do marvellous things nowadays," Pearl said with desperation, the tears falling down her cheeks.

"We both know that's not likely, don't we?" Edward smiled at Pearl. "I've been the luckiest man on the planet to find you and I'm so happy you agreed to become my wife. That day I offered to buy you a drink at the dance – remember? I nearly didn't! I'm still not sure where I got the courage from – the beer probably, but oh, my darling, I am so, so glad I did. We have had the best life I could ever have wished for and I love you with all my heart."

"Well, you have made me the happiest I have ever been, sweetheart, and I love you too!" Pearl was openly crying now, the tears unchecked. Susie came back in and Edward asked her to ring Pete and get him to come in.

They sat at his bedside and held his hand as he drifted in and out of consciousness until at ten thirty p.m. that night he passed away. He was seventy-four.

Pearl was numb for weeks afterwards and she was grateful Susie and Pete had organised everything for the funeral. It was all a blur for her, and she was glad her children and Ruby were there to take care of her.

"I know now what you went through when you lost dear Derek," Pearl said to Ruby one afternoon as they sat with a cup of tea in Pearl's kitchen. "Although, in a way it was better for me because I did get to say goodbye, I suppose," she mused.

"Yes, sweetheart, definitely and he wouldn't have wanted to linger on for months and months declining in front of you – that certainly wasn't Edward!" Ruby said soothingly.

"Are you going to carry on living here? I know how hard it is with all the memories."

"Yes, I've spoken to the children. I don't want to move in with them – as nice as it would be, they have their own lives to lead and I want to be here – close to Edward, you know?" Pearl couldn't bear the thought of leaving the home she had shared with that wonderful man. She felt as if their lives were incorporated into the walls and the furniture.

"Susie and Pete have taken his clothes and whatnot to the charity shop, so they might help someone and it's something I couldn't face doing."

"That's sometimes the hardest part, isn't it? Remember when Derek went? You started to pack up his shoes and you broke down; Tony and Jack lost it when they were going through his shaving stuff! It's the little things that make the whole person, that's what is so hard, I think," Ruby said, still feeling the loss of Derek even though she was now married to Colin and they were happy.

"I always thought I would go first," Pearl said. "Edward never seemed to be ill, not even when the children were small and had cold after cold. I don't think he ever really recovered from the chest infection or maybe the cancer had already got him by then!"

"He certainly never seemed to have any time off work that I remember. He was always fit and healthy, but then Derek seemed the same," Ruby said.

"Right!" Pearl said, jumping up, "I'm not going to sit here weeping and wailing for ever – let's have a glass of wine. Edward would want me to be happy and I'm certainly going to try!"

"To Edward!" They raised their glasses and toasted to him. "To us!" Pearl cried. "Friends to the end!"

"Friends to the end," Ruby echoed her.

Pearl lived in her home for a further eight years and she had carved a life for herself without Edward. Susie and Pete were a massive support to her as was her dear friend Ruby, of course.

Just after her eightieth birthday in the May, Susie and Pete gently broached the subject of her maybe selling the house and moving into a retirement home. She was reluctant at first, to say the least! She valued her independence, but she was well aware that she wasn't able to cope as well as she used to. Various things around the house needed to be done and she knew she was becoming a bit forgetful. She was terrified of leaving the gas on and all the other myriad things that came with old age.

She agreed to go and look at the retirement homes and after two or three they all settled on Willow Lodge; it wasn't too far from where she used to live, and she instantly felt 'at home' there.

Chapter 34
August 2018

Tony adjusted the collar on his shirt and glanced at Jack who was looking a bit pasty faced. "Christ, I'm not looking forward to this are you?" he said. "What's up with the tissues? You haven't got a cold, have you?"

"No, I think its hay fever," Jack said blowing his nose noisily for effect.

"Hay fever? You've never suffered from it before!" Tony looked mystified then it dawned on him. "Ah, I wish I'd thought of that! Good reason to keep wiping your eyes and nose in case it all gets a bit too much, hey?" He patted his brother on the back as they waited for the taxi bringing Ruby to the pub. "It will be all right, bruv," he said reassuringly. "We didn't think of this happening, though, did we?"

The children and grandchildren had decided it would be a great idea to give Ruby a little send off for her trip to Switzerland and had organised a lunch at the pub as a bon voyage to her. As they had decided not to tell them the real reason for Ruby's trip Tony and Jack could only go along with it and pray no awkward questions were asked. They both felt guilty for keeping the truth from their families, but Ruby was excited about it as she thought it was an excellent way to say 'goodbye'.

"I just hope I can keep it together for Mum's sake, hence the hay fever cover," Jack said with a grimace. "If it all gets too emotional, you know?"

"Yep," Tony said, "It's not going to be easy, but it will only be for an hour or so I reckon. Mum gets tired easily these days so once lunch is finished, we'll get her back to the home and settled in and the kids will be happy they've treated her."

The taxi arrived and they helped Ruby out of the back seat; Jack sorting out her sticks and Tony positioning the wheelchair as the dining room was at the back of the pub and she would have trouble walking all that way. Ruby looked lovely in a dark blue dress and jacket and she had had her hair done and, although she looked a little frail, her eyes were sparkling, and she looked the happiest her sons had seen her in a while.

"I'm so looking forward to this, my darlings," she said, as they wheeled her through to the restaurant.

The rest of the family had arrived and after the usual greetings they all went in and found their table. Jack went back to the bar and organised the drinks as Tony helped his mother to her seat at the head of the table.

Tom, Karen, Oliver and Megan were there with Will and baby Alice on one side with Jake, Claire and their sons Max and Jake Jnr alongside them. Kirsty and Jordan sat with Maddie and her boyfriend Matt on the other side with Tony and Jeannie and Jake and Maria sitting on either side of Ruby. Once all the orders had been taken and the waiter had left Ruby started to speak.

"Well, my dears, first of all, thank you so much for organising this lovely lunch. It means a lot to me to have you all together with me before I leave for my trip." Ruby beamed at everyone and thought how lucky she was to have such a wonderful family. "As you know, I'll be leaving next Wednesday and so I won't see you again before I leave, although Tony, Jeannie, Jack and Maria are obviously coming with me, so I think this calls for a glass of bubbly, don't you?" She looked at Tony who signalled the waiter to bring over the champagne. While everyone was cheering and toasting Ruby's health, Jack was overcome by a coughing fit and quickly left the table. When he returned, the waiters were setting down the meals and there was the usual chatter as everyone started to eat, so he was able to slip back into his seat quietly and Ruby's hand clasped his for a moment as she looked into his eyes. The love for him was shining from her liquid eyes and he managed a weak smile and squeezed her hand back in gratitude and to reassure her he was alright.

"More champagne, Mum?" Tony asked, holding up the bottle.

"Ooh, just a tiny drop more please, darling. The tablets I'm on don't really like me drinking but I do love the bubbles, don't you?" She laughed as he poured some into her glass.

In the end it was a lovely afternoon and they were all relaxed and enjoying themselves; the food was amazing, even though Tony and Jack just picked at theirs trying to find an appetite.

"So, what else have you got on your bucket list, Gran? Besides going to Switzerland; a trip in a hot air balloon or maybe sky diving?" Jake laughed and the others were quick to suggest more daring things for Ruby to do to tick off her list.

"Ooh, I know, Gran, how about white-water rafting?" Maddie suggested, laughing along with Ruby as she said she wasn't sure what else she wanted to do, but who knew? She would write them down and let them know if she decided to go with one of their suggestions, but only on the understanding that they had to do it too!

"Ah, well, that's me out!" said Kirsty. "I can't see the point of getting soaked through and the chance of being flung out of the boat – not my idea of fun!"

"Well, I'm sure you will enjoy Switzerland anyway, Gran," Tom said, holding on to a wriggling Will as he was trying to get down and run around the table. "All that lovely fresh mountain air will do you a power of good."

Ruby hugged him and said she was looking forward to seeing the mountains with snow on the top at this time of the year – but only from her window – she certainly had no plans to climb one!

Oliver, Megan and the children left first as Alice was getting a bit fractious and needed a nap. As Tony watched them kiss Ruby goodbye and she cuddled her great-grandchildren, he could feel the painful lump of emotion stuck in his throat as he knew this would be the very last time, they would ever see her, and it was breaking his heart. He felt Jeannie's hand find his under the table and he clung onto it like a lifeline.

After another half an hour or so Ruby was starting to flag and whispered to Jack that maybe it was time for her to return home. There was a flurry of activity as everyone wished Ruby well again and said their goodbyes. Tony found Jack outside in the garden of the pub taking deep breaths; he could see his shoulders heaving as he struggled to gain control.

"Mum's nearly ready," he said gently behind Jack, giving him time to compose himself.

"Okay, I'm all right. Just give me a minute and I'll be there," Jack said and turned to give Tony a watery smile. "I couldn't face seeing them all say goodbye; that was the worst bit!"

"Yeah, me too. Once the taxi has taken Mum, we're going to go over and be with her for a bit. We won't be long as she looks exhausted, but after that I've still got half a bottle of that twelve-year-old single malt if you're interested?" Tony thought they could probably do with a good stiff drink later.

"Sounds like a plan, mate!" Jack said as Maria came out to find him. "All right, love?" he asked, knowing how hard this was for her and for Jeannie too.

"Yes, it went better than I expected, and no one suspects anything odd, I don't think. They all just think this is your mum's last hurrah for a holiday and a tick off the bucket list. It went well and your mum has had a lovely time, that's the main thing." Maria hugged him and they went back in to get Ruby organised.

"Oh, my darlings, that was so lovely, thank you so much." Ruby was settled in bed now and could see the tension in her sons' faces ease. "I know how hard this is for you all," she said encompassing Jeannie and Maria with her smile, "But to be able to say goodbye and tell them all I loved them was such a comfort to me and although this won't be the last time, I just want to say how much I love you all too." Her eyes were shining now with unshed tears as she drank in their faces. "I understand how bad you were feeling keeping the truth from them, but I honestly think it's better this way. They won't be worried about me and their last memories of me will be that wonderful lunch and get together; that's what I want them to remember."

She clasped her sons' hands and her grip was surprisingly strong as she said, "You have always brought joy to my life and my love for you is eternal, never forget that, my darlings. Now! Before I start wailing, you all run along, and I'll have a nap. The champagne has gone to my head a bit, I think! Oh, by the way, before you go, would you ring Susie or Pete and let them know I'll be ringing Pearl on Monday afternoon about three ish, please? She has the hairdresser coming in, but she thought she would be done by then – if it changes, can you let me know?"

"Yes, Mum, of course. I'll ring them tonight and we'll let you know tomorrow," Tony said.

They kissed her and hugged her and left her to sleep, her eyes already fluttering closed as they gently shut the door.

In the end it was Jeannie who rang Susie when they got back to her and Tony's house. The boys were working their way thought the whisky and she opened a bottle of wine for her and Maria; Maria said she would only have one glass as she would be driving home later.

"Sure, you're welcome to stay you know, we have the spare room all made up ready if you wanted a glass or two?" she said.

"I think one of us with a hangover tomorrow will be bad enough, but thank you anyway," Maria said wistfully. She could do with a drink herself, but it would be better if Jack woke up in his own bed – assuming she could get him in it!

"Yes, you're right, but if you change your mind the offer is there. I might just have the one glass to take the edge off, you know. I'll ring Susie first, though," Jeannie said, picking up her mobile and scrolling through her contacts to Susie's number.

"How did it go?" asked Susie gently when she answered her phone. She knew they were going out for the lunch and had been thinking of them all afternoon. "How was Ruby? Did she enjoy herself and how did you all manage?"

"Ah, well you know, it was okay. Both the boys struggled a bit, but they were brilliant and no one else seemed to pick up on any tension, I don't think," Jeannie said taking a welcome sip of her wine. "Ruby had a marvellous time and she had two glasses of champagne, so was a bit merry by the time she got back and is now in her bed having a snooze!"

"Ha, ha! I remember Mum always saying Ruby loved a glass of champagne – she loves the bubbles! Maybe we should... no, sorry, that's completely inappropriate... forget I said anything." Susie was mortified by what she had been thinking.

"Were you going to suggest we have champagne afterwards darlin'?" Jeannie said, which was exactly what *she* had been thinking, but wasn't sure she should say anything to Tony.

"Well, yes, it was, but, well, does it seem so wrong?" Susie was relieved Jeannie had been thinking the same thing.

Maria looked over at Jeannie and gave her a big grin and a thumbs up!

"Ah, sure and Maria thinks it's a great plan as well!" Jeannie said, grinning herself now.

"Maybe we should see what Tony and Jack think before we start carting around magnums of the stuff though? Oh, Dan's here and he thinks it's a brilliant idea too!" Susie said cautiously.

"Well, it'll have to wait until tomorrow before we get any sense out of those two!" Jeannie said and went on to tell Susie about the boys and the whisky and the date set for Ruby to ring Pearl.

"I don't blame them, to be honest. It will do them good to let their hair down a bit tonight and get it out of their systems a bit. Are you girls having a drink too?" Susie asked, confirming that Pearl was having her hair done at eleven a.m. and would definitely be finished by the time they were ready for a natter.

"Well, we are on our first and possibly last glass; Maria is going to drive Jack home later. I've offered to put them up here, but Maria thinks Jack will be better off in his own bed." Jeannie was halfway through her glass of wine and topped it up thinking, to hell with it, she might as well have another.

"Okay. Well, let me know what they say about the champagne and we'll get something organised. I'm sure Pete will be up for it, so if Tony and Jack are okay with it, we'll do it!" Susie said goodbye and Jeannie ended the call.

Maria and Jeannie chatted and finalised some of the plans for the coming week, discussing what was appropriate to wear to go to the clinic and deciding Ruby wouldn't be happy if they turned up all in black!

"I think we should just wear something cheerful as if we were really on holiday," Maria said. "I've got a nice dress that's summery but not over the top, so I think that's what I'll wear," she said, mentally going through her wardrobe.

"Good idea. I'll do the same and I'll check with Susie, so she doesn't feel left out. I should have asked her just now but didn't think of it until you mentioned it. Not to worry, I'll call her tomorrow. Now, I guess I'd better check on those two and see if they want some cheese and crackers to soak up some of the booze!" Jeannie said, getting up.

Ruby woke up after an hour or so and she felt a bit woozy, but decided it was worth it after the lovely day she had had. She thought back over the afternoon and was sad to see the pain in her boys' eyes. It was the first time in weeks that she had nearly wobbled and backed out of it, feeling selfish as she knew it would be Tony and Jack dealing with the aftermath. Although most of the funeral plans were sorted, they would still have their grief to deal with and have to be supportive to their children and grandchildren. She wished there was a way she could spare them the pain and suffering, but she told herself that, even if she didn't go to Switzerland, there would come a time in the not too distant future when she would die anyway and they would still be in the same situation.

She thought how strange it all was that people still treated dying as a taboo subject; yet, it was going to happen to everyone so why not have the death you wanted rather than wait for the inevitable end and run the risk of leaving behind someone you didn't say 'I love you' to?

The one thing she was grateful for was that she hadn't had any bouts of forgetfulness lately. She *had* forgotten Maddie's boyfriend's name, but Jordan had spoken to him and said his name – Matt! That was a relief and she hadn't let herself down at all.

One of the carers came in with her tea as she had decided to stay in bed and not bother getting up to go to the dining room tonight. She felt better after eating something and was enjoying a cup of tea and a programme she liked on the TV.

Chapter 35
September 1937

"Come on, love, you don't want to be late on your first day, do you?" Mavis Williams helped her daughter button up her coat and stood back to admire her. "You look lovely in your new school uniform, I'm sure you will make lots of new friends there."

"I wish we hadn't had to move, Mum, I really liked my old school and I'll miss Jane and Elizabeth, but I'm excited too!" Ruby was feeling nervous about being the new girl, but it was the start of the new term so there would probably be other children in the same boat she thought.

"I know love, but Dad has started this new job and it made more sense to move into Norwich so he can get to work easier and as he's getting a bit more pay – and I'm not promising mind – but there might be the new bicycle you wanted from Father Christmas this year. If you're a good girl, of course, and get all your homework done!" Mavis said, hugging her daughter as they made their way up the road to the school.

"I'll be the bestest girl in my class, you'll see!" said Ruby as she hopped and skipped alongside her mum.

Fifteen minutes later they were in the headmistress's office waiting for Ruby's teacher to take her to the classroom she was going to be in.

"Ah, there you are, Miss Masters," said Miss Talbot. "Now then, Ruby, this is Miss Masters and she will be your teacher for the whole of this term. Anything you don't understand or are not sure of be sure and tell her, all right, dear?" she said kindly. Ruby looked shyly up at her new teacher.

"Hello, Ruby," Helen Masters said. "I'll take to your classroom and we'll get you settled in. Say goodbye to your mum for now and you will see her again at half past three," she said, giving Ruby and Mavis a warm smile.

"Yes, Miss," Ruby said, her voice wobbling a bit for the first time.

"Have a good day, love, and I'll see you later. I'm making your favourite fruit cake for tea as a treat so it will be ready when you get home." Mavis and Ruby clung onto each other and Mavis watched her small daughter being led by the hand off to her new class with tears in her eyes.

"Settle down, everyone," Miss Masters said. as they entered the classroom. "Everyone, please say hello to Ruby. She is joining us this term, so I expect you all to be nice to her and help her with anything she needs."

The children all looked at Ruby and said in unison 'Hello, Ruby'.

"Now, let's see. Hmm, I know, I think we'll put you next to Pearl – two precious gems should be together, I think!" Miss Masters gently guided Ruby to where Pearl was sitting in the second row.

Pearl thought Ruby was the most beautiful girl she had ever seen; she had the loveliest shining chestnut brown hair brushed and tied back into a ponytail and her eyes looked like chocolate buttons. She hoped Ruby would like her and smiled as the new little girl sat down next to her.

Ruby was glad she didn't have to sit next to a boy and looked at Pearl, taking in her blonde hair and huge blue eyes. Pearl's hair was in a side parting with a bow tying back her fringe, framing her heart-shaped face. Ruby was pleased to see Pearl looked friendly and she could see the sparkle in Pearl's eyes. She suddenly gave Pearl one of her huge grins and Pearl grinned back at her – and that was it! – They were inseparable from that moment on. They could hardly wait for the lunch break and spent the whole hour talking and laughing as if they had known each other for ever. Their friendship deepened and Ruby was so, so glad she had now moved to this school. She vowed to give her dad a big hug when he got home from work to say thank you to him for getting his new job.

Chapter 36
August 2018

Pearl was sitting in the lounge waiting for Ruby to call her. Her hair was done, and she was pleased with the result, as always – Sheila always seemed to be able to get Pearl's hair looking thicker and more lustrous. She applied her lipstick and settled back in her chair thinking this would be the last call they would make before meeting up in Switzerland the day after tomorrow – for the last time.

Her emotions were all over the place. She was excited to be going away with her children and Dan – it was a holiday for her after all – but underlying her excitement was the dread of the real reason they were going. She still hadn't been able to make up her mind about the final day, but Susie had reassured her and said she didn't have to decide until the last moment. Dan would be with her and would do whatever she decided.

She was almost ready to go. Jill had helped her sort out what to take and her case was just about packed, Susie was going to come in tomorrow and sort the last few odds and ends out for her – toiletries and any last-minute things she needed. She had a list of things to bring back; Arthur had said he liked chocolate and she was going to get some for him, Ted and the other carers. Poor old Hilda couldn't have any. 'Not with my innards dear!' she'd said when Pearl had asked her if she would like some. Susie had said they could look around and get a little something for her from the local shops, and there was always duty free to wander around while they were waiting to fly. Pearl wanted to get Jill something special and she was thinking maybe a bottle of perfume might be nice.

Suddenly her Kindle sprang into life and there was Ruby's lovely face on the little screen.

"Pearl! My dear, how are you?" Ruby was smiling at Pearl and, even though she was looking frailer than the last time they spoke, her voice was still clear, and her eyes were shining. "Your hair is looking lovely, as always."

"Hello, sweetheart. I'm fine thank you. Yes, Sheila is marvellous," she said giving her hair a little pat. "How are you, dear? How was your family lunch?"

"Oh, it was wonderful! It was so lovely to all get together; it was the best gift they could give me." Ruby told Pearl all about the food and the 'bucket list' the grandchildren and great-grandchildren had teased her with, "Ooh and, Pearl, we had some champagne! Do you remember how we always loved a glass or two of bubbly?"

"Oh, yes, you loved the bubbles! Mum always used to say that champagne was for special occasions, but Edward said where you were concerned every occasion was special if a bottle or two were opened!" Pearl said, fondly remembering her friend's love of the wine.

"Ha, ha! Yes, well, why drink ordinary wine when you can have champagne? So much more glamorous, I think. I used to think it made me look sophisticated!" Ruby laughed.

"You were always sophisticated, sweetheart, so much more than me anyway." Pearl was laughing too now.

"Never! I always wanted to be like you. You had this kind of, I don't know, poise about you that I envied and tried to emulate all the time!" Ruby said, surprised that Pearl didn't think she was sophisticated. She had always wanted to be like Pearl, with her blonde hair and her heart-shaped face she was the epitome of glamour and she knew Edward had thought so too.

"Really?" Pearl was incredulous. "But I always wanted to be you! It's taken more than eighty years for us to tell each other how we felt, and we thought we knew each other so well." Pearl's eyes were sparkling, and she had a broad grin on her lined and wrinkled face, making her look to Ruby just as she did when they were at school together.

"I know!" said Ruby, grinning back. "Anyway, I'm so glad we became friends all those years ago. I was thinking about the first day I met you the other day, do you remember? When Miss Masters sat us together?"

"Oh, yes, I was so pleased she did. I was dreading who was going to be in the empty seat next to me, then when you came in and was looking around shyly, I was desperate for her to see me sitting alone and bring you over and I couldn't believe it when she did just that!" Pearl said, her mind going back to that September day eighty years ago – near enough to the day, she thought – her smile slipped a little as she thought of all the years that had gone by and now here, they were nearly at the end.

"We have had some wonderful times, haven't we?" Ruby said, almost as if she was thinking the same as Pearl – which she probably was, Pearl thought.

They chatted some more about family and how the new additions Olivia and Alice were getting on, until Pearl could see Ruby was looking tired and she was struggling a bit to remember who Pearl was talking about sometimes. They ended the call, and both said how much they were looking to seeing each other in a day or two. It was only afterwards that Pearl realised neither of them had mentioned what Ruby was doing there; it was if somewhere along the line they had both come to terms with it. Pearl could see now it was the best thing for Ruby and her family in the long run and she was happy, in a strange kind of way, that they had been able to have this time to spend with her and make the memories they would cherish in later years.

The following day Ruby said a tearful farewell to the residents and staff at High End; it had been her home for the last few years and she had felt comfortable and very well looked after there. Tony had come to collect her, and they left to a chorus of 'safe travels' and 'have a lovely time' and 'see you soon'. The journey to Tony's was quiet as they both were deep in thought. Jeannie was waiting at the window as they pulled up and Jack and Maria arrived just as they were helping Ruby out of the car into the house.

They had enough time for a sandwich and a cup of tea before they would leave for the airport.

Pearl was thinking of her friend as she and Susie packed the last of her things in her case. Pete was going to pick her up in the morning and she would spend the night with Susie and Dan before she, too, left for Switzerland. Pearl couldn't imagine how Ruby must be feeling as she did everything for the very last time; the last goodbye, the last car trip, the last flight. She was finding it difficult enough and *she* was coming back!

Susie sat with her for a while as they talked softly about it and Pearl could see Susie was as upset and emotional about it as she was.

Jill embraced Pearl and hugged her in the morning. "Bye, bye, love. I hope you have the best time you can and please give my love to Ruby." Her cornflower eyes were clouded with unshed tears. Pearl was like a grandmother to her and she was extremely fond of the old lady who had come into her life ten years before.

The other residents had all said their goodbyes and old Ted looked crestfallen that the time had finally come for Pearl to leave. "Have a good holiday, I hope the flight's not a bugger!" he said gruffly, trying to keep his emotions in check. "Come back safe and sound and tell us all about it."

"I will, Ted, I will," Pearl said. She was quite fond of the silly old fool in her way and she would miss him, but she would be back in a few days and she would regale him with – nearly – all the news.

They arrived at Susie's and she said that Tony had called to say they had arrived safely and were looking forward to meeting up with them the next day. It was a strange evening as they talked about everything that would be happening; from the flight to the arrival at the clinic on the Saturday. They explained to Pearl the idea about having some champagne to toast Ruby as Tony and Jack had thought it was a fitting tribute to their dear mother. Pearl told them again about Ruby's love of the bubbles and the mood lightened as they all shared their memories of the wonderful person Ruby was. Pearl was relieved that they had once again reassured her she didn't have to make any decisions until the last possible moment, and she was looking forward to spending a couple of days sight-seeing and spending time with her dear friend.

The flight was uneventful, and they all arrived safely early in the afternoon. Tony and Jack came to their hotel for a drink; they said Ruby was having a nap and they arranged to meet up for dinner at the hotel Ruby was in as it was easier for her not to travel about too much.

The two old friends were overjoyed to be reunited and after dinner they sat side by side on a large sofa in the lounge area, the others sat around in the comfortable chairs and Pete ordered some drinks from the bar.

They discussed their itinerary for the next two days – Ruby's health permitting – and the following day they were going to see the Rapperswil Rose Gardens. There were around one hundred and fifty varieties of roses with a special fragrant rose garden area for visually impaired and disabled people to enjoy – it was quite flat there and Ruby would be able to get about in the wheelchair. They were then going to take the one-hour boat ride along Lake Zurich where they would be able to go to the Lindt chocolate factory in Sprüngli; Pearl would be able to buy her chocolate gifts from here to take home. Tony had hired a people carrier which they would all fit in and the clinic had loaned them a wheelchair for Ruby. He said they could hire another one if Pearl thought she would need it, but she assured him she would be all right so long as they took it slowly.

On the Friday they were going to go to Bahnhofstrasse for a little shopping and in the afternoon, they were going to visit the Fraumünster church.

Pearl and Ruby were thrilled with the planned trips and their children were pleased they were able to fill the days for them – it would also take everyone's minds off the visit to the clinic which was always lurking in the background of their minds.

Chapter 37
September 2018

Pearl woke up with a start. She looked around at the wallpaper in her room and slowly realised where she was and what today was. Today was the day! Susie knocked gently on the door and came in to get her up and ready for breakfast.

"Hi, Mum, how are you? Did you sleep?" She looked at her mother, trying to gauge her mood. She could see her eyes were red rimmed where she had obviously been crying the night before.

"Morning, darling. Yes, I slept really well – surprisingly. I think it's all that sight-seeing over the last two days we've done. I think Ruby has enjoyed it, though, don't you?" Pearl was aware of Susie's gaze and said, "I'm all right, darling, don't worry. Have you heard from Tony this morning?" Pearl was almost dressed and ready by now.

"Yes, he rang to say they were going to the clinic for the last round of visits to the doctors and for Ruby to get settled in," Susie said, her throat almost closing with emotion. They had seemed to talk about nothing else except this day from when they had first found out and now here, they finally were – it seemed as if nothing would be the same after today. Susie couldn't even imagine how it was going to be tomorrow when they said goodbye to Tony, Jack and the girls as they left them behind to deal with the official paperwork in relation to Ruby.

They made their way down to breakfast and saw Jeannie and Maria sitting at the table with Dan and Pete. Pete was pushing his meal around on his plate until he finally gave up and pushed the plate away.

"The boys were the same, Pete," Maria said. "None of us could stomach any food, we just sat and drank coffee." She lifted her cup and said, "This must be my fourth cup and it's not even nine a.m. yet!"

Pearl managed a small slice of toast and then asked the question they all wanted to know the answer to. "What time will it take place?" she managed to say before her voice disappeared.

"It's at around eleven ish. That was the time Ruby has chosen, although of course she can, er, well, you know, it could be half past if she wants." Jeannie broke down then as she thought of her dear mother-in-law and how they were going to have to carry on for the rest of the day.

"Now, Mum, we are going to leave for the clinic at ten, but Dan will stay here with you, unless you want to see Ruby for the last ti… er, again." Susie broke off, unsure what to say.

Pearl and Ruby had shared a final embrace the night before and a tearful Ruby had said she would completely understand if Pearl didn't want to be at the clinic. Pearl was equally broken hearted as she kissed her friend and said she just couldn't decide. They separated reluctantly and Pearl went to her room early and cried until she felt her heart was going to break.

"I've decided I'm going to stay here, darling, if that's all right?" Pearl looked at Susie and Dan nodded his acquiescence.

"Yes, of course, it's fine and if you change your mind Dan will get you there in plenty of time so it's entirely up to you." Susie got up and hugged her mother, realising how difficult this was for her and them all.

"We are going to get off then." Jeannie and Maria took their leave and they both hugged Pearl and said they would see her later. They were keen to get to the clinic and support the brothers.

After everyone had left, Pearl and Dan sat in comfortable silence in the lounge with some tea and a plate of cookies watching the comings and goings of the small hotel.

Ruby had been given the final go ahead, as it were, and she was settled in her room; an intravenous drip was set up in her left arm and the plunger which would administer the fatal dose was lying on a tray by her right side. She was chatting softly with Tony and Jack and holding their hands as the clock on the wall silently ticked down the countdown to eleven. The tears coursed down Jack's face now and he made no attempt to hide them or brush them away.

"I love you so much, Mum. I hope I've made you and Dad proud over the years and I want to thank you for being my mum." His knees buckled and Tony just managed to catch him and sit him in the chair next to Ruby's bed.

"My darling, I couldn't be prouder of you any more than I am at this very moment and I know Dad is waiting for me and he is nodding the same." She smiled at Jack and looked up at the ceiling as if she could see right through to the heavens and see Derek.

Tony took the seat the other side and he too was crying openly now. "Sorry, Mum, I promised myself I wouldn't get all upset and here I am blubbing away."

"It's perfectly fine, darling. It shows how much you care about me and you know I feel the same way. This is really the best way when you think of it; having these precious moments to say what we want and share our emotions, don't you think?" Ruby's eyes were glittering with tears for her beloved sons. Surprisingly, though, she was calm and not a bundle of nerves as she had thought she would be. In fact, she would go so far as to say she almost felt numb; it was as if all her emotions had shut down and she was left feeling almost serene.

Jeannie and Maria arrived with Susie and Pete and they hugged and kissed Ruby. She looked around expectantly and sighed as she realised Pearl wasn't with them.

"Mum's okay," Susie said softly. "She sends all her love, but…" She broke off.

"I understand, darling. Will you tell her I love her too, although she knows?" Ruby smiled gently at Susie.

A nurse came in to check on Ruby and take her temperature and blood pressure. She left and soon returned with a tray with coffee and tea and placed it gently on the side and said if they needed anything to press the bell and she would return.

Pete had an overwhelming urge to press it and ask them to stop the whole process but restrained himself.

Maria busied herself pouring drinks for everyone and they resumed their seats to wait.

Pearl was watching Dan as he kept glancing at his watch and checking his mobile phone,

"What time is it now, dear?" she asked him for the fourth time in the last ten minutes.

He checked his watch again, even though it only had only been a few seconds since he had looked.

"It's ten forty-five." He sighed softly and moved around on his seat; he was perched on the edge of his seat and he could feel his legs starting to go numb.

"I do hope Ruby is all right," Pearl murmured almost to herself. Her chest was tight, and she was overcome with emotion. She suddenly sat up straight and said, "Dan, I need to be there, can we get there in time?"

Dan jumped up and said, "Yes, of course." He grabbed the car keys and helped Pearl into the passenger seat of the car, relieved to be doing something at last.

Ruby looked up at the clock and said softly, "It's time, my darlings." The gentle strains of Vivaldi came through the speakers and Tony got up to pass his mother the tray with the plunger on.

Jeannie, Maria, Susie and Pete hugged and kissed Ruby one last time then stood back to let the brothers be by their mother's side as she was about to take her last breaths. Tony pressed the buzzer to alert the doctor who slipped discreetly into the room and stood quietly in the corner.

A sudden flurry of activity outside the door stopped everyone in their tracks and Ruby, with the plunger in her hand, looked up to see what was going on.

Pearl pushed open the door and took in the scene in the room. They all stood as if they were statues frozen to the spot, and she looked past them all to see her dear friend in the bed – still alive!

"Oh, my darling Ruby, I'm so sorry, I should have been here." Pete helped Pearl to the chair Jack had jumped up from when the door had opened.

"Hello, darling. I'm so glad you are here, although I understood if you couldn't. Now, it really is time. Please look after yourselves and know that, even though I may not be with you, my love for you all is eternal and will never die." She picked up the plunger once more and gazed lovingly at her sons, she said softly, "I love you, my darlings." She looked at Pearl, who was distraught, her eyes huge and round as she sat in disbelief. "My darling friend, I love you – friends for ever – remember?"

She closed her eyes and pressed the plunger.

The doctor certified her death at 11:06 a.m.

Jeannie and Maria went outside with Pete as Susie waited for her mum to leave. Tony and Jack kissed Ruby and left the room to do the initial paperwork. The doctor had said there was no rush and the room was theirs for as long as they needed, but they both had to get out for a few minutes; they could come back and sit with her in a little while.

Pearl looked up at Susie and said, "I'm so glad I was here in the end, darling."

"Yes, Ruby was so pleased you were here, and I think it will be good for you later to have known you were with her at the end, Mum," Susie said. "Do you want to go back to the hotel and have a lie down or something?"

"Do you know, I think, if it's all right with the others I might just sit here for a bit and talk to her. Is that okay?" Pearl said. "Oh, and, sweetheart, would you fetch my bag from Dan's car please? In all the haste to get here I left it on the passenger side floor – it's my lipstick you see, I want to put a last bit on for Ruby – she used to tease me about it so much when we were younger."

"Yes, of course, do you want me to get Pete to sit with you until I get back?" Susie opened the door.

"No, I'm fine; I'll just sit here and chat to Ruby." Pearl smiled at Susie.

"Okay, I'll only be a minute then." Susie hurried out to the car park to fetch Pearl's bag.

Pearl sat with her friend in silence. She looked up and there was Edward smiling at her; she took his outstretched hand and felt his fingers close around hers.

"Here you are, Mum. Do you want me to get your lipst... Mum? Mum? Are you all right? MUM!"

Epilogue
Christmas Eve 2018

They all stood in a circle in the field, laughing and stamping their feet to keep warm,

"Right!" said Pete. "Here goes!" and the cork flew out of the bottle with a loud POP!

They all cheered and held out their glasses for a glass of the champagne they had brought for the occasion.

Simon, Tom and Jake were setting the stake in the ground and Tom said, "Okay, we're almost ready here."

The firework was ready to be fired and they cleared a space so it could rocket off to the heavens.

Susie thought back to that fateful day when she had gone back into Ruby's room and seen Pearl slumped to one side. She had called for a doctor and afterwards thought how ironic that was considering they were in the clinic! The doctor had said Pearl had had a massive heart attack and pronounced her dead at 11.20, only fourteen minutes after Ruby had passed.

The following days were a nightmare of grief mixed with the protocol of Pearl dying in a foreign country and all the bureaucracy that ensued. Eventually they had decided it might be better all-round if Pearl was cremated with Ruby and they could bring back their ashes together.

Simon had said he knew a company which made bespoke fireworks and maybe it would be a nice idea to keep a little of their ashes after the scattering ceremonies and send them off together in a rocket. Ruby's family all thought it was a wonderful idea and it would truly be a fitting tribute to the two old friends.

"Okay, countdown from five… four… three…two… one… FIRE!" they all chanted as Tony lit the blue touch paper and the rocket was launched. They watched as it gained height and there was an enormous bang and a cascade of white (Pearl) and dark red (Ruby) starbursts lit up the festive sky.

"CHEERS!" They all chinked their glasses with one another, "FRIENDS TO THE END!"